ELIJAH

CALHOUN MEN BOOK 2

KATHI S. BARTON

World Castle Publishing, LLC
Pensacola, Florida
Copyright © Kathi S. Barton 2016
Paperback ISBN: 9781629893891
eBook ISBN: 9781629893907
First Edition World Castle Publishing, LLC, May 2, 2016
http://www.worldcastlepublishing.com

Licensing Notes

Cover: Karen Fuller
Editor: Eric Johnston
Editor: Maxine Bringenberg

CHAPTER 1

Helenia stood in front of the mirror. She liked this new look. The younger people used so much color in their lives that she was sure that they'd had her in mind when they came up with it. The pink of her blouse, the green of her pants…she thought perhaps that she could get used to this style, unlike the other decades when women wore long billowing clothing and wigs that itched. Not to mention shoes that pinched so badly that she would sometimes go barefoot under her clothing so no one would know. Not that she cared, but it still gave her a sense of freedom. And Helenia was going to be free forever.

She was still trying to decide which other outfit she was going to keep when she felt the movement of air around her. Standing as still as she could, pulling shadows from every corner around her to hide herself, she turned and looked around when she knew no one could see her. Not humans at any rate.

"Hello, Helenia. It's been a very long time." Dante flicked at her shoulder when they both knew there was nothing on her. When he did so again, she grabbed his hand and held him tightly in her grip until he dropped to his knees. "You always did overreact. Let me go, Helenia. I do not care for being treated this way."

"Perhaps you should have thought of that before you touched me." She bent his hand back more until she heard the bones break. His screams went unnoticed by her and the patrons of the store. They were invisible to anyone but other supernaturals. "What are you doing here? You know that I do not like you well enough to have you around me even for a moment."

"They're hunting you." She let him go and asked him who was hunting her. "The Board of Vampires, they're looking for you. They have every vampire looking for any information about you, and there's a bonus if they have an idea where you might be staying."

"And you? You thought to collect on it, Dante? I should hope that you're smarter than that. To know that to try and profit off of my demise, you'll be dead before the next sunset. I have no more use for them than they do for me. I like it that way." She looked around and saw that two others were watching them, vampires younger than Dante and not even close to being anywhere near as old as she was, and far less powerful. "Did you come with others? To hope to trap me?"

He stood then, his wrist healed already, and looked to where she was looking. He must have fed before coming to catch her, she thought, but it would do him no good. The two others, both males, started toward them.

"I don't know them. They more than likely heard about the bounty on your head, and decided to collect too." She asked him how much it was. "Twenty-five thousand points."

"So much?" He nodded. "And all for me? What do they think is going to happen when they send babies for me? That I shall sit idly by and let them take me in?"

Vampires for the most part had no use for money. She had a great deal of it; over the centuries she'd managed to steal a great deal of not just cash, but gems and other valuables that humans used. But after a while, usually after a couple of centuries, a vampire would realize that having it for no other reason other than it was easy to come by held no appeal. She had hers to get humans, stupid animals, to do things for her.

So the Board had been giving out points, or credits, to use when they had committed some crime or had not followed a rule in the strictest sense of the word. Helenia had long since stopped trying to gather points. She was so far in the hole now that even if she got a thousand a day, it would not put a dent in her bad deeds.

"Noah is after you as well." She looked at Dante just as the two babies, the younger vampires, were closing in. "He is the one that called the Board on you, from what I understand."

"I thought him dead. He is such a pussy, even for as old as he is. Christ, to think that he finally grew some balls and turned me in. Not that it will do any of them any good. I am stronger than he is by far." Helenia hadn't had any dealings with Noah, but she knew what he was. A vampire that stayed alone and followed most of the rules.

The babies were nearly to her when she lifted her hand and blasted one of them with her power. He was nothing more than ash on the shoes of the people who continued to walk the sidewalks in the mall as if he'd never been. She supposed, as far as they knew, he had not. The second man, stupider than the first, lunged at her, and she simply snapped his neck. If this was the best that the Board had, she was going to live for another thousand years, easily. His ash dusted the outfit that she had on.

"I swear to you, Dante, there is no hope for nice things anymore. I get me something pretty to wear and these idiots just come along and mess it up." He said nothing but looked around. She wondered if he was expecting more babies to come for her, and just grabbed three of the outfits she'd been looking at and left the shop. Dante was right behind her.

"What do you plan to do? Go back to your lair?" She said nothing as she moved in and out of shops picking what she wanted and sending it to her home across town. It was much easier than going around with a large bag in her hands, and it wasn't as if she needed to keep any receipts. Helenia hadn't paid for anything in decades. "I was wondering if you need someone to be with. I'm between homes right now."

"Do you suppose that these shoes will match the dress that I got? No matter." They disappeared as well. "No, I don't want you around me. I prefer my own company to that of idiots."

Two more stores, mostly clothing then a jewelry store, and she had all that she wanted for now. Honestly, Dante had soured it for her by telling her about the Board. She turned to him when he asked her again where she was going now.

"I should have thought that you'd know better than to try and collect on my being jailed, my friend." He tried to look shocked, but it looked mostly like fear to her. "To think that after all this time, you still think me stupid. When all along, it was you."

Helenia let her magic go and let her body return to its true self. She felt empowered by it, the shield off her face and her body released. Dante started to step away from her, but she put her long claws into his chest and felt his beating heart. When he cried out, she pulled his heart from his chest, feeling the power of it like a shock to her system.

"So pretty, don't you think?" She wanted him to see her eating it, taking the still warm thing to her mouth, but he disappeared, just like the other two had. Frowning, she dusted the ash off her hands from his heart when it, too, was gone. "Did you honestly think that I'd tell you anything, you moron?"

Going to her lair, she put the things that she'd taken in the trash. Like her outing today, they'd been ruined by Dante and his news. She could think of any number of reasons that the Board was after her, but it didn't really matter. Helenia lived by her own rules. And soon she'd be in charge of everything, including the humans, and it wouldn't matter at all what they wanted. She looked at her calendar and realized how long it had been in years since that night. He would be ready for her now, her blood rendering him weak enough that she could take his seed.

It seemed longer when she thought of the last time that she'd seen him. An alpha. Watching him all night long with the people he'd traveled with, she knew that he was going to be the one to help her create an army of monsters like her. Helenia smiled. She was under no delusions that she was anything but a monster. She had worked hard in creating herself to be one. And now that she was perfect, she wanted to make more in her image. And the alpha was going to help her.

Everyone knew that wolves carried a gene that was far superior to any other shifter. Vampires had it as well, in great abundance. But a wolf also had the ability to shift and to be stronger still with his other beast. It was this beast, the wolf, that she was counting on. Her creations would be wolf beasts, and she would control them all.

Making her way to the labs that she'd set up years ago, she knew that the man she'd put there, Basil something, would still be sleeping. He'd been asking to go home; his family apparently couldn't do anything without him there. And if anything had happened to him between then and now, she'd have to start all over. So putting him into a deep sleep had been better for everyone, mostly for her own peace of mind. And his family was no longer around to make demands on him, so that had been a plus for both of them.

As she made her way by one of the big buildings, she saw an ad in the window. Staring at it for a long time, she finally stopped someone to ask them the date. There was no way she'd messed up that badly.

"October tenth." She told him to tell her the year and when he answered her, she nearly fell backward. It hadn't been one year as she'd thought, but four. Fuck. There was no telling what her alpha had gotten into since then.

~~~

Noelle was intimidated by the big office, mostly because of the guards in the lobby. They were big and armed. Not that she planned on doing anything wrong, but she had a fear of men that were big.

But she was running out of time and this man, the one she was coming to see, had been the one that had come up on her search as the most trustworthy. She hoped so. When she stood in front of the big desk, she had to clear her throat twice before she could make any sound come out of her mouth. Nerves were making her sick.

"I'd like to see Mr. Calhoun please." The woman asked her if she had an appointment. "I do. For today at ten."

It was just shy of nine, but Noelle hated to be late. When the woman asked her to have a seat and that she'd call him, Noelle went to sit on one of the big chairs that looked like a family of five could have used. She watched the people coming and going.

An older man came in and started talking loudly about the weather. She was sure that he talked that way all the time, loud and with a great deal of humor. And everyone here seemed to know him. He stopped by the desk as she had, but he wasn't asked about appointments but sent up to the elevator with a smile. Noelle wanted someone to like her that way.

Noelle had, for the most part, been alone all her life. She worked and socialized when she had to, but she preferred her own company to that of other people. It more than likely was because of her family and the way that they'd jump out of the smallest places to hurt her.

When her name was called, Noelle made her way to the desk. It was just after nine-thirty by then, and she had to pee. But this had to be done today. Mr. Calhoun's secretary said that this was his last appointment before December, and that would be too late. Going up in the elevator with the guard, she held tightly onto her plastic bag and hoped she was doing the right thing.

"Hello, Miss Alexander. Mr. Elijah Calhoun isn't in yet, but his brother Trent is. He wanted to know if he could help you." She knew that name as well. But he was no longer working here, she'd heard. Noelle asked her about it. "He helps out when necessary. And since Elijah is running slightly behind, he thought he'd help him out."

Nodding, she was shown into a large office. As soon as she saw them, the older gentleman and the big man behind the desk, she wanted to run. They were too much and too big. Noelle turned to leave and the older man spoke.

"Come on now, sweetie. You're not gonna deny an old man a chance to sit with a pretty girl, are you? And Trent here, he is just glad to see me today because he won't have to eat all them delicious biscuits that his lovely wife made

11

him. I'm his daddy, TJ Calhoun, and we're about as harmless as they come." She looked at him, then at the steaming plate on the desk. "Come on back and have a seat, and let us see what we can do for you."

"I won some money." She didn't know why she'd blurted it out like that. Noelle had been holding that secret for five and a half months now. "I don't want anyone to know that I did."

"All right then. Why don't you have a seat and we'll figure this out?" Trent stood up, and she moved closer to the door behind her. When he sat down, she watched him carefully. "I won't hurt you, Miss Alexander. I promise you that."

Nodding but still not moving, she wondered why she was even doing this. She'd been making it on her own, without the money in her bag, for years now. This money, all of it that she'd won, would make it better for her, but she was terrified of what it might bring too. But to have a house of her own with a yard was something that she'd been thinking about for years.

Making her way to the chair, she sat with her bag in her hand and tried to think. "I was sixteen when my stepfather left me at a party. He and my stepmother had other children of their own, and they felt that my check from the welfare office would suit them better if they didn't have me around needing any of it. Sucking them dry is what they said I was doing to them." She glanced at the elder Calhoun when he made a noise, and felt her face heat up. He asked her how she was both their stepchild. "My mom died after marrying him. Then he remarried a few months later and she had children of her own. I didn't know it at the time, but they were his children, both of them. Ron is twenty now, and Daniel is two years older. I'm telling you this so you understand why I'm...I'm afraid, Mr. Calhoun. I don't want them to come back and try to hurt me again."

"You think they will?" She was sure of it and said as much. "I see. And this money that you won. I'm assuming that it's a great deal. That it's not just a scratch offs."

"I have those as well. When I would win some money, I would put it back in an envelope until it was close to expiring. I never cashed it all in, just enough to get by on. It was my emergency money, I guess. Every week I would buy one scratch off and one of the bigger lottery money tickets. I haven't stopped that since I won. The article I read at the library said to go about your business like nothing happened. So I did." He asked her how much she'd won. "The Powerball. I won the one from five and a half months ago."

Neither of them said anything for several seconds. Then TJ laughed, and looked at his son when Trent asked him what was going on. His dad was still laughing as he explained to Trent.

"She won the big one. The forty-million-dollar jackpot, didn't you, love?" She nodded and dug the tickets that she wanted to cash in from her bag. "Holy milk balls, Trent, she's the winner that they've all been looking for."

She looked at Trent when he asked her if that was true. "Yes. I won and I have to turn in my ticket or it's going to go away." He took the envelopes that she'd put into the plastic bag she used as a purse most of the time. It was all she had to carry it around in, and felt silly for it being so mundane. "I read about your firm at the library and everyone said that you can be trusted. I don't want anyone to know who I am."

"All right, let me look a few things up here. Just...I have to call in our attorney to help me get this right for you." She shook her head, but he said it would be fine. "It's my brother, Tanner Calhoun. Did you read about him too?"

"Please don't make fun of me." She wanted to snatch her things back from him, but he stood up again and she sat still. "I've never hurt anyone. I work and keep to myself and don't bother any of them. But they come and take whatever I have on me and then beat me for it. I'm not sure what they'd do about this money. More than likely kill me." She looked at them both before speaking again. "I've changed my mind. I don't want the money."

When he sat in the chair next to her, she whimpered. Men, big ones, scared her. Trent didn't move, but TJ got up and walked out of the room. She had no idea what he was going to do, probably call the police now that they had her tickets, but she didn't care. She wanted to go back to her place.

"You say your family takes your money and they hurt you? Have you ever called the police? Filed a report on them? We can do that now if you want, Noelle. I can do it for you." His voice was soft, full of something that she'd never heard from anyone when they were talking to her. Compassion. "Tell me so that I can find them and beat the living shit out of them. My wife, Joe? She'll have to visit me in jail, but I think she'll think it was worth it to see you safe." She laughed when he did. "There you go. See, I might be big, but I'm as gentle as a puppy."

"My stepfather is Howard Merrill. My stepmother wasn't any better. Her name was Gloria Merrill, but she died a few years back. I think she was in a car accident or something. I can't afford the newspaper all the time." She looked at Trent and felt...she wasn't sure what she felt except no longer afraid, for some reason. "He thinks I made him lose his job. I guess in a way I did. But when he lost his job, he lost everything else too. Like my government money. He didn't get his pension either, which I suppose is the way it should be with him being fired and all."

"You think that he'll try to take your money that you won." She nodded, then shook her head. "Ah, so you think that he'll take your life while he's at it."

"He will. Like I said, he feels that I owe him for some reason. He's not been happy with me for a long time." That was an understatement. "I have a place that I've been living in for a while. But I want my own home. A yard. I really want a yard."

"I understand that more than you can imagine. I've talked to...had my dad talk to Tanner, and he's on his way in. He works for a friend of ours, but he said he'd help us out. I know investments better than I do the letter of the law for this sort of thing. And my wife is coming in as well. She said that she was going to come by today, and she should be here soon. I want to try and get this worked out for you so that you can get you a house as well as be safe."

"I know what you are." He said nothing, and she looked at her hands in her lap. "I know that you and your family are wolves. I can't always tell what a person is, but I can tell when someone isn't human. I am, but I know that you're not."

"No, I'm not. Are you...is that why you're afraid of me? Is your stepfather a wolf?" She shook her head and told him that her family was human as well. "But one of them hurt you, a wolf or some other shifter."

"Yes." He didn't pry, and she didn't feel it was necessary to explain. He was going to help her get her money, and that would be the end of their relationship. "There are other tickets too. Not as much as the big one, but I'd like to have that money as well. It's what I can pay you with."

"I'm not going to charge you for helping you, Miss Alexander. I think you've been hurt enough." She wanted to cry, to beg him to hold her. There was something so comforting about him that she wanted to let him take care of her. But she knew better than to trust that kind of feeling. "Tanner is here. I don't want you to be alarmed when he comes in. He has a tendency to not knock, but to come in like he's been shot from a rocket."

The door to the office slammed back against the wall. The man who came into the room was talking, as if whatever conversation he'd been having with Trent the last time he'd seen him was still going on. He spoke to Trent about changes in the market and how he was getting his office set up slowly. He looked at her and stopped talking.

"Well, hello there. Aren't you about the prettiest little thing?" She shook her head and felt her fear double. "I'm sorry. I didn't mean to embarrass you. But you are very pretty. I'm Tanner Calhoun. Trent said you need someone to advise you on some lottery winnings."

When he sat down on the edge of the desk, she had a feeling that Trent had told him to back off. Tanner grinned at her before he asked her about the ticket. She knew then that she might be able to do this. These men wasted no time in getting to the point.

After he was shown the ticket, he asked her a lot of questions about it. The other tickets, mounting to just under ten thousand dollars, were given to the secretary to verify. Tanner said it wasn't as if they didn't trust her, but they wanted to make sure they weren't going to have any problems when they were taken in. The big ticket was put in a safe so that no one could take it from her now that a few people knew about it. A copy of it was made for her to keep, as well as a receipt stating that they had it in their safe for her.

"Does your stepfather have any idea that you've got any money? I mean, from your winnings? Did he lend you money for anything? Pay your rent somewhere, or any of your bills? At any time, did anyone help you out with a bill or something?" She told Tanner no, that she didn't tell anyone. "And your bills? You paid those with your own money, nothing ever coming from him?"

"I've made sure that I made my own way. I've never been on welfare either...I promised myself that I'd be independent as much as I could. And my stepfather was better at taking than he was at giving. Never the tickets. I never had them on me when they, my stepbrothers or him, found me." She looked at her hands again. "My stepbrothers weren't like that when I lived at home with them. They were spoiled, but they never bothered me. I'm still not sure that they do this because they want to."

"I'm sorry about that. No one should treat anyone badly, especially not a female. But knowing that about him makes it so much easier now. And the fact that you bought it after you left home and were out of his care means he has no claims on it at all. Those are things that I want to keep from happening."

For the next hour she went over the paperwork. By the time she was finished, not only was she exhausted, but she was also richer. The money from the tickets had been taken all over town and cashed in by different members of the family, so that nothing was ever going to come back on her. She'd never had so much cash on her at any time in her life. And then Joe, Trent's wife, showed up.

"Hello, Noelle. It's been a very long time." Noelle looked at the door, then back at the woman who had been there the day she'd been kicked out of her family. "Don't. Please don't run. Noah will be so happy to see you."

"He won't." Joe said that he would. "I hurt him that day. He might...he'll want to hurt me back."

"No, he won't. He looked for you for years after you left. And he'll be glad to see you, I promise." She looked at the door again, wondering if it was too late to take it all back. "I know your scent now, Noelle. You won't be able to hide again. But I promise you, Noah never wanted you hurt by this either. I'm not sure how you think you hurt him, but I've spoken to him. He's glad to know that you've come back around."

Terror like she'd not felt for a very long time skimmed along her skin. Her hands hurt from clenching them. Her head hurt from trying to sort through all the things that were running through her head. She'd hurt Noah because her father had been an important man in his business. Howard had told her that when and if he ever found her that Noah would make her pay for making one of his best employees have to be fired.

The door opened again and she screamed. She had no idea who might have come in or why, but her terror was too much. And when someone grabbed her, Noelle lost whatever hold she had on her fear, and the darkness swallowed her up.

CHAPTER 2

"I don't suppose you can tell me much about her." Elijah had come into his brother's office to see a woman falling apart. He supposed that they had it under control, but when she looked at him and screamed, it was all he could do to hold onto his wolf. Then he grabbed her before she fell to the floor. Trent didn't answer him, so he looked at his dad. "Dad? What was she doing here today?"

"Won the Power Ball and came in to see you about getting it cashed in. I guess the fates have a way of working things out for us." Elijah wasn't so sure about that. He looked at her again as she lay on his couch in his office. "You wanna tell me again how you don't think she's your mate?"

"Dad." Trent looked at him when his dad laughed. "Why don't you go and see what the progress is on the ticket? And see what Joe has to say about this girl. The fact that Noah and Joe know her makes me think that there might be more to this story than she even knows. This stepfather of hers, we need to find out as much as we can about him as well. We don't need him coming around trying to stir up trouble for her or us."

His dad was still laughing when he left them. Elijah didn't want to talk to Trent…he just wanted to sit there and think. Right now there wasn't much going through his mind but the fact that she was his. But he needed to think about what he was supposed to do with her now.

"You want to know the story?" He said that he wasn't sure. "All right. I'll tell you what I know for sure. As you know, she won the Power Ball a few months ago. And since she only had six months to claim it, she came here to have you work on how to make it happen. All she wants out of this is…well, other than to be safe, she wants a house with a yard."

"I think she can afford it. But I have a house for us." When Trent didn't say anything, he looked at him. "What? I do. You know that I bought one a few years ago. I don't live in it but occasionally. I have one that we can live in together."

"I'm not sure you get it yet. She wants her own home, with her own things with her own yard. I think this is a dream of hers." Elijah said he was right, he didn't get it. "Would you like to know what her address is?"

"What does that have to do…? Yes, where does she live?" Instead of answering him, Trent handed him a sheet of paper. It was a form that they had new clients fill out to put contact information on. "No phone, no cell. And this address is…Christ."

"Yeah, I thought that would ring a bell. The place has been set for demolition for about six months now. But she is using it as her home. At least her address. She might only be telling us that so we can't find her." They both looked at the couch. Then Elijah looked at the rest of the form.

"She works. It says here she makes pizza for the local pub downtown. That's not far from where the building is. Have you sent someone to look to see if she resides there?"

He said that he'd sent Scott. "And what did he find out? Anything?"

"Don't know. He said that he was taking pictures and that he'd be in shortly. I have no idea why, but that's what he said." Elijah nodded and wondered if she was living in one of the apartments there. "He made it sound as if she's not the only one that uses it as a home place."

"So she's basically homeless." Trent said it would seem that way, or she was off the grid. "Because of this family that she has. Do you think that Noah knows who they are? That he might have some information on what happened to her?"

"You could just ask me." Elijah stood up when she spoke. When she sat up, she swayed a little, and he moved to help her. He'd never seen anyone dizzy while sitting before, and worried that she might not be eating well. "I'm all right, thank you."

Elijah sat on the couch with her. He knew that she was nervous—hell, so was he—but his wolf was happier if he was closer to her. When she glared at him, he smiled. He kind of liked her show of temper.

"I live in the building you were talking about, and I pay rent. I'm not sure why you'd think I was homeless." Elijah looked at Trent and then back at Noelle. "What is it now?"

"We own that building. Well, I do. But I don't have any tenants in it that I'm aware of." She nodded. "No. I'm not sure what's going on, but I'm not renting it out. We've had it in the works for a few months now to tear it down and build some much needed condos in its place."

"But I pay rent to a company by the name of Windshield. They said that all the utilities were included and that trash pickup was also there. There are times when that's late, but we get it in our rent." She looked at her hands and frowned. "There are seven of us living there. I did wonder why no one else had moved in. But we're all paying nine hundred a month to stay there."

"I'll have Joe look into it. She can find out things faster than anyone I know." Trent got up to leave then and paused at the door. "You're not going to get to go back there, I'm afraid. Whoever is collecting rent from you is going to go to jail."

After he left, Elijah watched her. She was beautiful, he thought, her skin as pale as porcelain. Her dark hair was freshly cut…he could see small hairs on her shoulder and her neck. The thought of licking her there had him thinking of other places he wanted to taste her. He realized that she was saying something and asked her to repeat it.

"I said, what am I supposed to do now? I don't have anywhere to live." It was on the tip of his tongue to tell her that she could live with him, but he thought that he should take it a little slower on that score. "I have money, but not enough to buy me a house yet. And the money from the big ticket might take a little bit to get as well."

"Tell me about your parents and how you know Joe and Noah. And so you know, he's a friend of ours. And if Joe said that he's not mad at you, then I would take that as gospel. He's a good man." She nodded but didn't say anything. "I want to help you. I need to do this for you."

"You told your brother that I was your mate. I heard you say that when I was…before." He nodded and asked her if she knew what that meant. "Some. Not a lot. I know that you think I belong to you, but I can't. I'm not really the belonging to someone type."

He laughed. "And what sort of type would you say you are? And so you know, I think you're perfectly suited to belong to me." He watched her face redden, and he wanted to touch the skin to see if it was as hot as it looked. "Talk to me. If you don't, then I'm going to pull you into my lap and hold you."

"Don't do that, please. I have...I have some soreness." He asked her why, and she shook her head. "My stepfather worked for this company called Specktron. I'm not really sure what they do, but Howard, my stepfather, was one of the office men. Again, I'm not sure what he did there, but Noah Stark owned it. He told me that Noah had needed him there, that when he'd been fired it had been a big blow to his company, and that it was going to be years before they would be able to recoup the losses. I'm pretty sure he was full of shit, but Noah was angry that day."

"It's a company that goes to job sites, tells the person what it would cost from high end to low cost to do the job. Mostly it's buildings for big corporations. But they also look at land in different states and see what sort of tax breaks might come with building in certain areas." Elijah had just used them recently to see about a project he was going to look into helping out. "Noah owns several companies like that. Why do you think he's mad at you? If anyone, he was more than likely mad at your stepfather for whatever he'd done to you. I'm assuming that he was fired because of something that had happened and Noah knew about it."

"It was at his house that my...that Howard, Howard Merrill, decided to leave me." When she got up to pace, he let her. Not that he had it in his mind to stop her, but he wanted her to feel comfortable around him. "I knew they were going to do it. Not there, but that they were going to kick me out. I'd heard him talking to Gloria one night. But Noah had this party, a Christmas thing that he'd invited all his workers and their families to. I was sixteen then, and had never been to such a lavish place before. Noah had been making the rounds...Joe was with him. I think she was telling him who was who. He didn't come to the offices a lot...I guess because of what he is."

"Yes. Noah is a vampire." He tried to equate the man he knew now to one having a Christmas party. He was sort of a recluse, Elijah thought. "Had you ever been to one of his parties before?"

"No. But that doesn't mean anything. I mean, I didn't go a lot of places with the family after he married Gloria." Elijah was going to look into this as soon as he had enough facts. "Anyway, I was sent to the kitchen to see if Gloria could have something for her headache. I think I knew then that this was going to be it. And when I came back to where they'd been, they were gone. Even the van that we came in wasn't in the lot any longer."

"How did you involve Noah? I'm assuming that you did." She nodded and leaned against the wall. Elijah could see that she was still hurt by what had happened to her. And he didn't really blame her. "Noelle?"

"I went to find him. Him specifically. I think because he was really kind to me when we got there. He fussed over how...he said I was pretty. I'd not had anyone tell me that before." He started to tell her she was beautiful, but she spoke again. "I asked to use his phone. He unlocked his cell phone and handed it to me. But he didn't move away, just stood there as if he wanted to make sure that I didn't run off with it. When Howard answered the phone, he took the phone back and put it on speaker phone and nodded at me."

~~~

Noelle remembered the conversation like it was only a few minutes ago. Howard had barked in the phone, asking who was calling him. She'd told him it was her.

"What is it you want from me now, Noelle? I think, by leaving you behind, we've made it clear that we don't want you around us anymore. Hell, you're not of my blood or my wife's. The only reason we kept you this long is that we were afraid you'd die if we kicked you out, and someone would cut off that check of yours." She asked him what check. "The government pays us to care for your ass, believe it or not. And that money is going to go a lot further without you there sucking it dry. Not that you got much of anything anyway, but there was enough going in your belly that we had to give you. Now that you're older, we figured that you could fend for yourself or not. It really doesn't matter to us."

Noah had her ask if he was making enough at his job. "I don't understand. I thought you said you made good money working for Mr. Stark. You were even planning a long vacation with us."

He told her not her, never her. "And yes, I make great money working for that man. But there is always room for more, don't you think?" She asked him what she was supposed to do now. "I really don't care. But you're to never darken our doorstep again. Never mention us as being your family, and if I find out that you did, then I will hunt you down and make you hurt worse than I did before we left today. If I were you, I'd leave that house now before Mr. Stark finds out what sort of person he has there. A homeless bitch that no one cares for."

When the line was disconnected, she'd stood there. It wasn't until Noah had touched her that she'd screamed. The belt marks on her back were still raw from the day before when Howard had beaten her because of Ron's grade card. Not that she was sure how that had been her fault, but it never seemed to matter to him if she'd been involved or not. But she hurt when he touched his hand to her back. Lashing out, something that she'd never done before, she hit Noah in the face and bloodied his nose.

"I ran after that. I don't know where I thought I was going to go, but I knew that he was a powerful vampire and that I'd just hurt him." She looked at Elijah, who had said nothing while she told him what had happened.

"Noah fired him after that." She said that she wasn't sure how long after, but Howard had blamed it on her. "I would have killed him had it been me."

"Noah?" He said no, her stepfather. "You don't even know if I'm telling you the truth. No one else believed me when I told them that he was hurting me. The police even told me I was lying."

"I believe you. And I'll take care of him. And the police for that matter. I have a few friends on the force, and I'll get to the bottom of that as well." She asked him why he'd even want to bother. "Because he hurt you."

"That's no reason." When he stood up, she stiffened. "Don't hurt me. Please? I'll leave, but please don't hurt me."

"I will never harm you." His fingers moved down her cheek to her throat, and she shivered from the gentleness of it. "You're so beautiful. I know that you understand what I am, what we are, but do you know what you are to me? That you're my mate?"

"I don't have to be. I can just...I've been alone for a very long time, and I can be again." She watched his face when he smiled. "You look beautiful when you do that. It makes me think that you're used to getting your own way when you smile like that."

"Usually. But I don't think my considerable charm will work on you, will it?" She shook her head and was surprised when he laughed. "Are you going to be like this our entire lives, Noelle? Not letting me win any arguments when I try to charm you?"

"You are very handsome and a flirt. But I'm not as easy as some of the women you know. I do think you get away with things you do because of that." He asked her why she thought that. "I don't know. But I bet you have women falling all over you to do whatever you want, no matter the bullshit you sling around."

"You wound me." She felt herself warming to him, relaxing enough that when he touched his hand to her shoulder, she didn't immediately try to run. "Where did he hurt you, love? When I touch you, I don't want to hurt you too."

"He beat me with his belt, so mostly my back. You'd think as a grown woman that I'd be able to get away, but he...my stepbrothers help him." She looked up at him, wondering why she'd just told him that. "You're making me tell you, aren't you?"

"No. I can't do that to you. Not that I'd even try, but since you're my mate, I can't force you to comply with my questions or compulsions. You wanted to tell me. And I want to know." He asked her to turn for him. "I want to see how badly I'm going to make him suffer when I find him."

She turned, again not sure why she was doing this. And when he lifted her blouse up over her back, she felt the pain of the wounds when she tried to move away from his touch. He told her not to move, but she wanted to. So to cover her embarrassment, Noelle started talking.

"I was coming out of my work when he caught me. Daniel, one of his sons, hit me with something and I was down before I could think I should run. The ropes were on my wrists, and Daniel held me against his body with my arms up over his head while Howard cut my shirt off." Noelle moaned when she felt Elijah touch his tongue to her back. "What are you doing?"

"Healing you. Mostly tasting you. Christ, do you have any idea how much I'd like to shift and kill those men?" She started to turn, to tell him not to, when he pressed her against the wall with his hips to hers. "I'm licking them to heal them. My saliva has healing powers in it that will make them feel better. Talk to me. Like you were, talk to me."

"Ron, another stepbrother, he kept asking me for my purse or wallet." Elijah was making it hard to think. And when he asked her if they took her money, she had to concentrate on what he was asking her. "Yes. They used to. I don't carry money on me anymore. Nor do I have it at my apartment where they can find it. I have.... What are you doing to me?"

His body pressed against her, his cock at her ass, and she wanted to beg him to stop it, yet was afraid that he would. As his hands moved from her waist to her belly, then up to her breasts, Noelle wasn't sure that her heart was beating any longer. Her mind had certainly shut down. When he cupped her breasts under her bra, she leaned back against him and let him hold her up.

"I want to take you right here." She nodded, her body agreeing to things and her mind right along with it. "If I turn you around, I'm going to kiss you, strip you down, and then make love to you."

"You don't want to?" He laughed, and she felt her temper rise up. "I never asked you to do this for me, so if you're finished, I'd like for you to let me go."

"Never." As soon as she was turned, he took her mouth. It wasn't a kiss, only in the sense that their mouths were touching and his tongue was dueling with hers. But it was more, so much more, and she had to hold onto his shoulders or fall. When he cupped her bottom and lifted her, she cried out when his cock rocked into her pussy. "I need you."

"Yes." She wasn't sure that need was a strong enough word for what she wanted from this man.

"Christ. We have company."

"Company?" He nodded and continued to rock into her pussy while he held her to him. "I can't think when you do that."

"I can't think either. Except for the way that I'm going to kill the man on the other side of the door as soon as I can move." That's when she heard someone pounding on the door. There was laughter there, too...faint, but she could hear it. "It's Noah. Don't freak out, okay?"

"He'll hurt me." Elijah told her that unless he had a death warrant, he wasn't going to even try. Noelle looked up at him and could see his wolf racing over his skin. "You're going to shift?"

"No. He wants to mark you and isn't happy with the vampire that is keeping him from it."

She looked at the door when Noah said Elijah's name. "The sooner I let him in, the sooner I can get rid of him. I hate to put you down, but if I don't, I'm going to take you right here and to hell with him."

"Elijah, I would prefer that you waited on that. And I've not come to harm either of you. Could you please open the door for me?" Elijah growled and Noelle laughed. "Pretty please?"

It was really funny to see such a big man be so frustrated about something. When he kissed her again, she was set back on her feet, and he started to leave her. But he came back, kissed her again, and then went to the door. When he opened it, Noelle looked at the man standing there, Noah Stark.

"Hello, Noelle. My goodness, you are more lovely than I remembered." She looked behind her and he laughed. "You, my dear. You have grown into a very lovely young woman.

And I'm so happy to see that you have met your mate. Elijah is a good man. I could not have picked a better one for you myself."

"He's helping me." She felt her face heat up when she'd remember how he'd been helping her with her wounds. "His firm is going to help me with some things."

"Yes. I'm to understand that you've come into some money. Good for you. But as you know, that father of yours, he must be taken care of first. The little shit has been a pain in my ass for a very long time. We also have another matter to take care of as well. Nothing to do with you, but with your new family." She asked him what. "Helenia has opened her lab up, and I think I know now why she's set on getting a wolf in her clutches."

"I don't know who that is." She looked at Elijah when he only stared at Noah. "Is she working with Howard? Have they found out about the money too?"

"No. She's after my brother, Sterling." She asked Elijah how many brothers he had. "There are six of us, plus Joe and my parents, living around here. My grandparents are supposed to come.... Too much information, but I'm worried about this woman coming here. What about a lab? I don't think Sterl mentioned that before."

"Why does she want Sterling?" Before she got an answer, if she was going to get one, the room filled with people coming in. Noelle moved back to the corner of the room, as far from the group of them as she could get. But Elijah came to her and pulled her to him as he made his way to his desk. She thought for sure that he was going to help her out of the room, but he stopped and turned her to see all of the men and women.

"Everyone, before we get started, I'd like to introduce you to someone. This is my mate, Noelle Calhoun. We have a few things to work out yet, mostly me killing her family, but I'd like to introduce you to her." She nodded as each of them said their name to her, and was surprised by all the good wishes that were being given to them. "She's going to need us to watch out for her, as well as dealing with Helenia. Her stepparents are hurting her."

"I'm going to be okay." No one said anything, and she looked at Elijah. "I should go. You have a family thing going on and I should just go."

"You can't go back. Not to the place you were staying. Besides that, you are family now. I'm sorry, Noelle." She'd forgotten about that and looked at Trent when he continued. "I might suggest that you stay with one of us. Anyone volunteering to offer up a bed for her?"

The low growl from Elijah had her turning to him. It didn't frighten her, but seemed to make her feel warm all over. And when he pulled her body to his, all she could think about was how safe she felt. For the first time in a very long time.

CHAPTER 3

Helenia watched Basil as he moved around the room fussing with things. She wanted to ask him if things were going to work, but she didn't want to bring it up again. He had gone into such a state when she'd told him about the date that she didn't want to have to kill him to shut him up.

"You ruined it all." She started to ask him how it was her fault when he continued. "When the power was shut off, everything, including the samples that I had saved, were killed. The lab equipment that was running wasn't closed out correctly, and the freezers full of your DNA have been too warm for things to be viable. We're going to have to start all over."

"I don't think so. I've worked very hard in getting you everything that you need. Make it work." He said that there was nothing left to work with. Everything was dead. "I don't understand. You told me before I left you that day that it was ready to go. I only had to bring you the specimen and you could work your magic on him to make me the monsters that I wanted. You should have said that things had to keep going here."

She wasn't really sure why the power was off. It could have been because she'd not paid the power bill in over four years. Or it could have been the giant tree that was lying over the roof of the main part of the lab. Without her bothering to having it taken away or anyone watching over the place, things had fallen into disrepair. Even the larger house had been nearly destroyed when some sort of freak storm had come upon it.

"The computers are out of date as well. Even if I could get these up and running, there is the matter of the programs no longer being viable. And I have no way of knowing if any of the vats that I have set up in anticipation of this creature coming are still going to do what I want them to. Things are just...I just don't understand how you could have forgotten about the work we've done." She didn't either. "My family must think I've been murdered. My poor wife and children. I have missed out on so much of their lives because of you. If you could take care of getting things back up to running and I'll go and see them. I have sorely missed them."

"You have to stay here and work on this. I have no idea what to get to make this work again. Besides that, your family is all gone. They were a distraction for you and I took care of it." She looked at all of the equipment that Basil had deemed no longer useful. "Do you have any idea how much work it was for me to get this down here? Christ, it took me weeks of going back and forth between that other lab that I took things from and here. I can't do it."

When he didn't speak, she turned to look at him. Basil had sat down again at his desk, and she thought he was getting back to work. But he was staring at her, like he was unbelieving of whatever it was she had just done. Helenia started to tell him how she'd done it, brought him what he'd asked for, when he spoke.

"You killed my wife and children?" Frowning, she nodded. Now what have I done wrong? she thought. "Just went to my home and killed them because you thought they were a distraction? They were my family. All I had in the world. You can't have...are you really that unthinking of other people's feelings?"

"Feelings can get you killed. I don't even know why you're so upset with this. You were distracted. I couldn't get you to do your job correctly without you saying that you needed to do this. Some baseball game or some stupid school play. They're gone, end of story." He shook his head. "Now what? You'd think you'd be glad to have the noose from around your neck. When I went to see them, they were acting like they couldn't make a single decision without having you there. They were pathetic, Basil. You're better off without them."

"You don't get to decide that. They were my children, my wife. Do you have any feelings whatsoever about such things?" She told him no. "I can't work for you. Not now. Not after what you've done to.... You killed my wife and children."

"Yes I did. And unless you want to join them, I would suggest that you get to work." She let the façade of being normal fall away, letting her true self show to him. "I am in charge here. Get to work."

Her power was never fully hers as the other self. It sucked a great deal out of her to appear in a manner that didn't have people she needed to work with run for fear. She usually loved that feeling, the fear from humans, but today she didn't have time for this shit. It was well past time for things to move the way she needed them to.

"No." The single word was like a slap to her. Helenia felt her anger consume her as he stood there, his chin lifted up in defiance. She let her beast go completely. Even her thinking was normal now, no more trying to be anything but her evil self. Helenia smiled at the power that took her.

Her body grew to a much larger size. Her flesh tightened against her bones, and magic lifted her from the floor as she was eaten by her anger. She knew what she looked like to him, loved that even though he'd invited her monster to be free by telling her no he was regretting his decision.

Power shot from her fingers, elongated now with her true self. Her clothing fell away, her body no longer needing the conformity of them. When she touched him with her claw, tore into his throat with it, the smell of blood inflamed her power, gave her such a feeling of greatness that she let its warmth spray over her as his body bled out. She tore him to shreds then, her bare hands covered in his gore, his body nothing to her but a way to let her rage go. His heart was the last thing that she picked up. Taking it to her mouth, she ate it, feeling power rush over her for the freshness of the blood and meat. But she knew that the feelings wouldn't last long. It was getting harder and harder for her to get much of a thrill out of killing. That was why she needed to create her own army of monsters. It's why she needed the alpha to seed them with his abilities.

Helenia shot out of the building and took to the skies. It occurred to her on some level that she'd not just killed the man who was going to make things happen for her, but had destroyed her building as well. But the feeling of utopia was surrounding her, and she wasn't ready to let it go just yet. Seeing a group of people below her, Helenia dove at them, killing as many of them as she could before she took to the skies once more...simply lashed out at them with her claws, tearing into their bodies with her powerful anger.

She would pay for this rampage. Not that she cared about the loss of the lives of humans, but the power that she'd used drained her. And when she landed on the earth, her body covered in the sticky wetness of the dead, she dragged herself to her lair, falling several times on the way.

Smiling, she thought of the Board that Dante had told her about. She thought of Noah as well, and wondered what he would think of her killing so many of the cattle that roamed the earth as food for them.

"Noah has grown soft in his years." She lay on her bed, a slab of cold stone, and closed her eyes, thinking of the time when the two of them would come together. "I will defeat you, you bastard. There will be nothing to stop me from taking your life and your power from you."

Death began to take her. Her kind didn't sleep or even rest like other vampires did, as Noah did. But she died. Her heart stopped beating and all other functions of her body stopped. It was the way she loved it…no one could disturb her while she was in this state, nor could they find her. Helenia just ceased to exist.

~~~

Elijah read over the paperwork in front of him, but for the life of him he couldn't remember what it said. Twice now he'd tried to see what was there, but both times he'd been distracted by the woman that was currently going through his home…their home…and seeing if she wanted to live here. Not that it mattered to him where he lived so long as she was happy. That was a feeling as foreign to him as not being able to think straight.

"You should see your face right now. You look as if someone has just told you there was no Santa." Elijah growled at Noah, and the man laughed at him again. "She will be fine now. I'm so happy to find her again and to know that she's with the Calhoun pack. I did worry over her when she left that day."

"You said that you'd been looking for her. She was right here all along. What was the problem?" Noah leaned back in the chair and looked at him. "I'm sorry. I guess that did sound a little accusatory. But I'm stressed out."

"Of course you are. Your wolf wants his mate. I would imagine that you do as well." Elijah didn't even bother trying to deny it. "I wish to finish this, if you please, then you can take her to your room and show her what having a mate is all about."

"She doesn't trust us. I mean, me a little, but not the rest of us. And especially not you." Noah nodded sadly. "I'm sorry again. I'm not trying to make you feel bad."

"I know that as well." Noah said nothing for several seconds. "I didn't find her because I didn't look too terribly hard. I should have, I know this, but she wasn't with her family any longer and, though I knew that she was alive, I didn't know she was living as she had. And yes, I did fire her stepfather after I heard the way he...the things that she told you. Did she mention that they used her as their housemaid as well as live in sitter? Not only that, but she pretty much ran the household, did the cooking, cleaning, as well as kept the yard mowed and other things that a household should be doing together, not a single person."

"No. All she told me so far is how he'd beaten her the other day. You should have seen her back. I'm sure there are more marks on her than what I could see. It looked like he used the buckle end of a belt and it cut into her badly." Elijah had been shaken to his core when he'd seen her wounds. "She should have had medical treatment, not walking around trying to find a way to cash in her winnings."

"I'm sure that the money was much more important to her. It meant a way of life she'd not had until then. And perhaps she thought that with a home, she'd be safe. I know that when I have a place to call my own, I feel better about it." So did Elijah. "But about her stepparents. Her parents, what do you know of them? I know very little. Her mother died just about the time that Gloria was having her second child, both of which belong to Howard. But there was never any mention of her sire."

"I only know what she told me about her family and her stepbrothers. I'm not even sure she knows who he might be. About the brothers, she only said that they were helping Howard beat her. That one of them holds her down while he takes the belt to her. Do you have any idea what they might have done to her had they known about the money?" Noah nodded. "Christ, she has been living with the knowledge that she was a millionaire, while being beaten by the people that were to care for her. What a sick fucking world we live in."

"The day that she found me to use my phone, I thought even then that she was a beauty. Just so young and so afraid of life. I think...yes, I know that she knew what they'd been about. And when I listened in on the conversation between her and Howard, I knew then that she'd planned for me to know what he'd done." Elijah said that she had. "Very smart girl, don't you think?"

"I know that. But what I don't understand is why you say I can't go and kill them. I don't think there is a more deserving family than them." Noah told him it was about the money. "But we've already established that they had nothing to do with her winnings. And that they'd not supported her in any way that could come back to them."

"You know that, and we know that, but the public will not. Even if one person finds out that she won and then her family turns up dead, what do you think they're going to think about her? And her involvement? And with her being your mate so soon after their deaths and the winnings, what do you think they're going to think of you and your family?"

"They'll think that we planned it all. That she had them killed so as not to share in her money, and that I only married her for it. Or that I married her because we killed them together." Noah said that was it perfectly. "But none of that is true."

"Of course it's not. But do you think anyone wants to hear the truth when the scandal is so much better? People, humans I think, love to have drama in their lives. I do believe that they'd not be able to function should they not have a daily dose of it." Elijah thought he was right. He didn't have to like it though. "Marry her and close that door. Another will open. Her family will come forward then, wanting a piece of your money because of who you are. But if I were you, I'd not mention her money just yet. So long as she lays claim to it, she doesn't have to go public, correct?"

"Not in Ohio, no. She can claim the money and never have to have either her name or her face shown." Elijah had studied that part of it a great deal. "I have to convince her to marry me first. I don't think that is going to be all that easy."

"No, it won't." Noah stood up and smiled down at him. "But I have every confidence in you that you will persevere." The door opened to his office, and he stood up as well when he saw Noelle standing there. When Noah said that he was leaving, he turned and winked at him. He nodded to Noelle when he moved out of the room.

"I didn't mean to interrupt your meeting." He said that it was over. "Your butler, Mr. Casen, showed me around. He is very proud of the improvements you made here. He said that you've made the place a showcase. I have to agree with him."

"Casen has a tendency to over tell a story at times. And the only improvements I have made are the ones that he's nagged me about. He is quite the nagger, you'll find out." When she didn't move into the office any further, he got up to go to her. Seeing her stiffen, he sat on the corner of his desk instead. "Did you like the house? I like the place all right, I guess. And I have done some improvements on it, but if you don't care for it, we can look for something else."

"And you would do that, just on the say of me not liking this house?" He nodded. "That's not right. This is your home. You bought and paid for it. Made it look the way you wanted it to. Why would my opinion matter to you in anyway?"

"Because I want you to be happy wherever we live." She frowned at him, and he laughed. "What I mean is, this is not a home. Not to me. My parents' place is a home. My brother's place, that's a home too. Even the cabin that they stay at in the mountains, that's a home. But here? This is a place that I slept when I was too tired to go to the apartment I have in town. On occasion had a meal in. My family has been over a few times, but I think this place is cold. That is, until you got here."

"You think I warmed your house up?" He nodded and stood up. He moved toward her slowly so as not to scare her. "If I may be honest with you, this is just the kind of house that I had in mind when I won the money. I had much smaller dreams before that. A one or two-bedroom house, a big yard in the front and back. Trees, too, and a little garden in the back for me to grow things in. You're too close again."

"No, I'm not close enough. Not yet anyway." He kissed her gently but wanted more. "I'd like for you to warm this house up. Put a part of yourself here, pieces of your heart, as it were, around so that I can see that you live here with me."

"I don't have anything of my own." He nodded and moved her head so that he could nibble on her throat. "I don't have any books. Not a single plant. The furniture I had in the other place was things that I picked up at garage sales and auctions. I can't talk to you about this when you do that."

"Good. Since you came into my life, I've not been able to think at all, much less talk in a way that makes any sense." He picked her up in his arms. "Did you see the bedroom? I'd like to show you the bed right now. How bouncy it is. The way the mattress holds me up when I lay on it."

Her giggle had him pausing on the steps. He would bet his life savings on the fact that she didn't do that much, especially not lately. Elijah decided that he was going to make her laugh as much as he could from now on.

"I don't like sex." He nearly fell going into the bedroom when she made that confession. "I mean, I've not had it a great deal—once or twice—but it's sort of boring, don't you think?"

"Boring? Not if you do it right." He dropped her on the bed. "Maybe it's the guy you were with. He might not have known what to do."

She bounced twice before she sat up. "He said he did. Told me that women all over the world would line up to take him to bed." Elijah was sure that she was kidding and waited for the punch line. "After we were done, all I could think about was they must have been in the wrong line or something."

He couldn't help it, he burst out laughing. And when she laughed as well, he thought that he was seeing a side of her that few had seen. Or had bothered to see. Taking off his shirt, he talked to her about his wolf and what he wanted to do to her.

"I don't know what you mean by marking me." He nodded and told her that he wanted to taste her. "You mean like oral sex?"

"Yes. He would like to drink from you and take your juices into his body." She watched him and he her. Elijah wasn't sure she was going to go for it, and calmed his wolf with the knowledge that they had all their lifetimes to let him have her. "If you don't want to, sweetheart, he'll be fine with it."

"No, it's not that. I just never...it sounds like it would be good." He could tell that she was nervous, but she was excited too. "How does it work? Do we have to go outside so you can shift?"

He stripped off his pants and let his wolf take him. Elijah watched her carefully. Jumping up on the bed, he lay down beside her, putting his head on her belly. When her fingers touched his head, he closed his eyes, enjoying her touch as much as he did being near her.

"I thought you'd be rough. Your fur I mean. But you're very soft, aren't you?" When she rubbed him behind the ears, he groaned, and she laughed. "You're nothing but a big baby, aren't you? Well, you're beautiful, and I think I might just be in love with you as well."

Do you love me, Noelle? Her fingers stopped moving, and he looked up at her. *We can talk this way because I've tasted your blood. Do you love me?*

"I've never been loved, I don't think." Her hands moved over his head to his shoulders. "I'm not even sure what it is,

43

but this feeling that I have for you, even though it's only been a short time, is powerful. And I feel safe with you. All of your family really, but you mostly."

I do love you. Very much. And I'm very glad that we make you feel safe. You need to never worry about any of us hurting you either. We might tease you, but we'd never harm you. He licked her belly, and she giggled. *You have no idea how it makes me feel to hear you do that. Laughter is wonderful.*

"I need you." His wolf stood up. Elijah felt the connection he had with his other half, but at this moment it was different. Right now, he felt like the wolf was in charge of them. He couldn't even talk to Noelle, and that frightened him just a little. But he moved down her body to her scent, her heat, and Elijah felt his need. Snapping his teeth into her shirt, his wolf tore it off her. Then she helped him until she was naked for him.

Her legs spread for them. Elijah was hit with her scent like a slap in the face. His wolf growled low in his throat and Noelle put her hand on his head. As soon as he licked her from gate to clit, she screamed out his name. It was the best sound he'd ever heard, and his wolf loved it as well.

He ate her hungrily. Over and over he fucked her with his tongue, licked her thighs and pussy until she cried out that she'd had enough. But still he brought her over the edge, taking as much of her cream into himself as he could get. When he sat up, Elijah was surprised at how easily his wolf let him come back to himself. Now moving just as slowly, he leaned into Noelle's pussy and took over where his wolf had stopped.

"Please, no more. Please." Elijah slid his fingers into her while he suckled at her clit, watching her face to see the beauty of her release. And when she bowed up off the bed and let out a cry that had his wolf wanting to howl with her,

Elijah moved up her body, nipping and tasting her as he went.

She told him she couldn't come any more. "Oh, but you can. And you will. I want to feel your pussy wrapped around me. I want to release deep inside of you. Hear you scream out my name when I bite you."

He slid into her, his cock so hard that he moaned at the tightness. Fucking her slowly, kissing her mouth, chin, and throat, Elijah felt her hands at his back, her legs wrapping around his. Elijah wanted this to last, to bring her over and over so that the word boring never entered her mind when he made love to her. And when she screamed out his name, he watched her face, seeing the emotion, the beauty of it as it took her twice in the same moment. When she begged him for more, told him to fill her, he felt his balls tighten and his wolf snarl at him to finish. Elijah threw back his head and howled as he came as hard as he'd ever come.

Even as he emptied, he felt his need rise up again, his balls fill even as his cock thickened more. And when she tilted her head, offering him her throat, Elijah took it. He tore savagely into her hot flesh and drank deeply of her hot blood as he came again, holding her body to his, unsure if he was keeping himself from coming apart or her. And when he was empty, not just his balls but every part of him, he dropped atop her and felt sleep take him as he rolled to his back. His last thought as she curled around him was that he was never going to be able to do that again without dying.

CHAPTER 4

Sterl crossed the street with care. Just a couple of days ago someone had nearly been hit here when the driver was too distracted texting to keep an eye out for people. When he hit the other sidewalk, he kept running. He'd been making good time this morning, and hoped that it would help him sleep better.

He'd been having nightmares for the last several years. Sterl figured that nightmare was a mild term for what he was having, and they were more memories than anything. Memories of the night that several of his friends had been murdered and he'd been marked by a she-devil.

Nearly stumbling when he saw her face again, he had to pace himself a few steps before he felt like he could breathe again. Every time he thought of her, saw her in his mind, he'd remember what she'd done that night.

They'd been out, the five of them. His date had been sick that night, but instead of bowing out like he wished every day now that he had, he went along with them, bar hopping and having a good time. He didn't drink, not that it would have affected him like it did the others, but he had drunk some soda. He'd thought it was bad, so hadn't finished the drink before they left. He was sure now that it had been poisoned somehow. That it had been meant for all of them to be impaired.

The thing—he'd not known until recently what it was—had appeared out of nowhere, causing the driver, Mitch, to swerve to miss her and causing them to go over an embankment. Sterl was still fuzzy on how that had happened. By all rights they should have just gone into a ditch, not careened over the hillside, throwing them all from the vehicle and him into a tree. Then she'd moved from person to person to kill them, even going so far as to make sure that the ones that had not survived were really dead. She'd crushed Beth's—one of the sweetest people he knew—skull with a boulder too.

"Sterl?" He lashed out at the sound of his name. He'd not even realized that he'd run his five miles and was now on his own front porch, and that the man that he'd hit because he'd been deep in his memories was a friend of his. When he put out his hand to help him up, Michael took it but didn't let him pull him from the ground.

"I'm so sorry." Michael nodded but continued to hold his hand as he lay there. "I was thinking, thinking of things that I should leave in my dreams and not hurt people who have done nothing to deserve it."

"If you do not mind me saying so, you look terrible." Sterl nodded and pulled the man up. "I think I have someone that can help you. Well, she'll help, but she can be a bit much. I have called in a favor and she said that—"

"Oh, poo on your favors. I would have come anyway. My name is Myra. I'm an assistant to a very lovely and powerful witch. They're panthers, so if you smell a little feline around, that would be me." The woman was dressed in the most brilliant color of pink he'd ever seen. Not just her clothing, but her hair and the jewelry she had on as well. When she put out her small hand, he stared at it. "You will allow me to touch you, won't you, young man? I can help you in ways that you cannot imagine."

"I don't think so. Not yet, at any rate." She just grinned at him. "I need to go inside and get something to drink. If I invite you into my home, will there be consequences?"

"Well of course there will be." Her laughter made him smile. "There it is, that lovely smile that I knew was hidden somewhere deep within you. She hurt you, didn't she? The she-devil. Ripped into your heart and life as if you belonged to her, for no other reason than she wanted you. If you would allow me to, young wolf, I will help you in ways that you will not realize for years and years."

Sterl felt the effect of her words all the way to his feet. When he staggered back, his body just limp with exhaustion and fear, she grabbed him in her arms and helped Michael to practically carry him into his home. He was handed a glass nearly full to the top of a dark amber liquor. He handed it back to Myra, and she shoved it back at him, telling him to drink it down.

"I don't drink, and even if I did, it won't do anything to me. I'm not human." The woman just laughed and drank it straight down as if it were nothing more than a glass of water. "You do know that was about a hundred fifty proof, right?"

"Yes. Very nice. And I'm not human either, my dear boy. Now, let us get to the point here. You have someone after you that needs to be dealt with. I'm not saying that I can do it on my own, but we can work some of my considerable magic around the place to keep you safe." He nodded, then glanced at Michael, who was wringing his hands. "He thinks

I'm sexy. Young Michael has been after me to get with him for decades."

"I most certainly have not. Myra, I swear to you that I sometimes wish I had never saved you." Myra patted him on the cheek and asked him to contact Noah. "He said that he would be here when you have prepared the house for him. And you should also know that he is bringing the book with him. I think it will be most helpful."

"The house has been ready since you told me where we were going." She looked at Sterl. "It would be most helpful if you could call your brother Trent, as well as your father and mother. The rest will be brought here as well, but for now, we need to speak to them."

Sterl reached for his family, all of them. If this woman could help, even in a small way, he wanted them all to be safe as well. When Trent told him he was on his way, he told Myra. She sat across from him and asked Michael for a cup of tea, if he wouldn't mind.

"I'm to understand that you have no help here." He nodded, not sure where she was headed. "I have a few people I should like to place in your home. Just as a precaution. Alta is a wonderful woman that will cook for you. She's also a cook that can help you put your weight back on. How much have you lost?"

"Nearly forty pounds." She nodded as if she knew that. "I don't know what you think you can do. Noah has taken the poison away, and for the first time in years, I can shift and move without any pain. I'm not yet back up to my weight because I've been taking it easy."

"You're having nightmares that plague you even during the day. Your temper isn't what it used to be, and you've been avoiding your friends and family for fear of hurting one of them with your words. And on top of that, you've convinced yourself that you should have an operation that will take away your seed so that you cannot father any children." He felt his temper slide up over the edge of reason and his wolf snarl at him to kill. "You do and I will put you down, young man. I might give you the illusion that I am very laid back, but you fuck with me and I will hurt you in ways that Helenia might not have even thought of."

The tears, always there on the surface, seemed to fill his eyes. He hurt. Not physically right now, but all of him. He missed his family, his friends, and his way of life. He missed his students that he'd taught, the feeling of being around the younger people who were just starting out. Sterl let the odd woman wrap him in her arms as the gates to his emotions seemed to slide open.

Sterl was not one to cry. But he sobbed now, holding onto this stranger as if his very life depended on it. He knew that his thoughts were disjointed, just as his mind seemed to be, but he need to speak to her, needed to let her know what he'd been going through.

"She killed them. All of them, as if they were nothing. Tore them in half, crushed their heads with rocks. Even poor Beth, who was dead…she smashed her head into the ground so that her parents couldn't identify her." Myra asked him what she'd said to him. "Her nails were in my chest, and I wanted to just die then, but she held me there as if she waited for me to ask her to end me. I think…perhaps that is what made her pick me. That I didn't give up. You have no idea how every day I wished that I'd just died as well. Then she told me that I was going to be her biggest prize as yet. That my seed would flood the earth with demons."

"She had marked you before that. I'm sorry to say that she's not right in the head." He stared at Myra, and she grinned at him. "You have to admit that she didn't strike you as all there when she came to you, did she?"

"No." He wasn't sure if he was supposed to laugh or not, but she touched her fingers to his cheek and he closed his eyes. "I see her now. Staring back at me with her dead eyes. Every time I think of her, see her there, I see something more about her. Noah said that she wasn't really a vampire."

"No, she's not. A she-devil is not a term that we use lightly. There was no classification for her back when the Board was formed. Vampires are very strong, live a long time, and have for the most part the best ways of keeping track of people. People like Helenia. I have a book for you that I would like for you to read. It will help you understand the vampire ways of life, as well as some of Helenia. She is what we now know as a she-devil. A killer for no other reason than it makes her happy. What you saw that night is her true self." He looked at her when she took her hand from his face. When she nodded to the doorway, he looked too. "This is Alta. She's going to be staying here. You don't have to worry about her having a home to go to...she wants to stay in the little cottage at the back of your property."

"I don't have a cottage back there." She told him that he did now as the older woman served them up some tea. "I don't think...I've been out of work for some time. I get a little pension from teaching, but it's running out. I'm sure that I can't afford to pay anyone right now."

He had money, a great deal of it, but it was his stash...the money that he'd been putting back since he'd gotten his first job. That money had been earmarked for a larger house, one that would have had plenty of bedrooms for his children to live in, his family to use if they came to visit. Sterl realized that he should use it now. The family was never going to happen for him.

"No worries, Mr. Sterling. I've done well for myself, and I've no real need for money." He only nodded at Alta. "I hope you don't mind, but Myra said that I could make the kitchen area my own, so I enlarged it to suit my needs, and the pantry is now filled."

When she left them after pouring the tea and giving him a plate full of cookies and scones, he looked over at Myra. She was munching on several of the treats as she sipped her tea. Her clothing had changed, along with her hair. She was now dressed in plaid. Even her hair was marked with the pattern.

"You'll get used to me." He wasn't sure that was going to be possible, but nodded at her. "Ah, Noah is here, as is your father and mother. Trent is very close with his wife, Joe. Lovely woman, Joe."

The room was filled with his family before he could say anything. He looked at Trent when he sat beside him and asked him if he was all right. Sterl wasn't sure and said as much to his brother.

"I feel like I've been on one of those rides at the fair, where you know that it's all an illusion but you're not sure how it works." Trent nodded and laughed. "Myra said that she can help me. Help all of us with this woman."

"Do you believe her?" They both looked at the woman in question, who was currently talking to his dad and mom. Both looked as confused as he felt. "She has a way of making herself known, don't you think? I'm wondering if she makes her own clothing or she has to have a blind person make it for her. I don't think I've ever seen that shade of green before, have you?"

"It looks like pus." They both laughed, and Sterl felt some of his unease fall away. "If she can help us, then I'm all for it. I've been so terrified for so long."

"I know that, Sterl. We're all worried about you." Sterl knew that as well. He'd been worried about himself too. Things were not going well for him, and he needed it to be better. "Elijah and Noelle are on their way over now. I think they were sidetracked again. Having a mate is very exhausting, so you know."

Sterl didn't point out that he'd never find his so long as this threat was over them. Having offspring, even with a mate that had nothing to do with the devil that haunted him, still scared him. He wasn't sure that he'd ever feel comfortable being with a woman again after this.

"All right then, I guess that we're all here." Alta, his new cook, moved around the room as Myra called things to order. Everyone not only had a cup of tea or glass of water, but everyone had a plate of food. He wondered where it all came from, but knew that he'd never ask.

Noah started speaking when everyone settled down. "Helenia, as some of you might know, is not a vampire. She is what we know of as a she-devil. There are no male counterparts to her that we are aware of. Her evilness is what has made her live for as long as she has, and she is old. Helenia also has a great deal of power, but it's nothing compared to a vampire of the same age. Terror is what she uses to control people into doing what she wants, and it has worked well for her. Up until now. She does not drink blood to live. As far as I know, she needs nothing to sustain her. And as such, it has been difficult to make her abide by any rules set before her." Trent asked how much trouble they'd had with her before. "More than you can ever imagine. And it usually centers around her finding someone to father the masses of beasts that she claims to know how to control."

"I don't understand." Sterl started to tell his dad the story of what had happen to him that night...no one knew the truth of it but Trent and Noah. Now he assumed that Myra and Michael knew as they were here, but his family had never been told. "This person, she's coming here? For what reason other than us to kick her butt?"

"She wants Sterling here to father her beasts. Not sexually, though his seed will be involved. Her magic will make them." Trent looked around the room, then at him. "I'm not sure how it comes together completely, just that she needs him."

Everyone turned to Sterl, and he felt his anger get stronger. Trent touched his hand to his arm, and it was all he could do not to shift and kill him. When he told his wolf to back off, Sterl felt the walls of his control crumble. He blacked out, his body screaming at him to defend himself. Suddenly he found his head down between his knees and someone holding him there. It wasn't until he saw the shoes that he realized it was his mom.

"Hold him, Sterling James, or I will beat your bottom." He felt his wolf tear at him, and then his mom kicked him in the shin. "Hold him, or I swear to you that I'll stand you in the corner for the rest of your days. You're scaring me. Please don't do this."

Sterl held him. His wolf was pissed and wanted blood, but he only just managed to hold him back. When he told her he was all right, he sat up and looked around and noticed that he was seeing things in a haze. He looked at his mom and saw that she, too, was outlined in a red bloodied circle. He looked over at Trent and saw that he'd hurt him, badly.

"I'm fine." Trent didn't look fine, and they both knew it. "Just give me a minute, all right? I need a minute."

"I'm so sorry." Sterl had cut his face and arm. Trent was holding his arm too, and he could see that it might have been broken. When Myra stood in front of him, he looked up at the woman and could see her anger too. Sterl wanted to bow to her, give her his throat. "I don't know what's wrong with me. I want to kill everyone, including myself."

"Look at me." She stood there, and when he didn't look at her, she jerked his chin up and made him. When she stared at him for several seconds, he felt his wolf curl up, seemingly as if he were afraid of her as well. "I think we've been wrong about this, Noah. She's not just marked him, but she's controlling him. I can fix this, but it will be painful for the young pup."

"You do what you have to do." No one asked him what he wanted, and he was pretty sure that they wouldn't. Not that he didn't want this gone, whatever it was, but he thought that he should have some say over it. As he was ready to voice his opinion on the matter, he felt the touch of someone in his head.

You'll fight them. Tell them that you belong to no one but me. He looked at Myra when her grip on his chin tightened. *Fight them all. Kill them. You belong to me.*

"She's there. I can see her now. Sterling, you just hang onto me now and we'll get you safe." He didn't want to be safe, he wanted to kill. His wolf was no longer in the corner but pacing in front of him as if to say, "Let me at her." "Noah, we might lose him if we don't act now."

"Take him."

Sterl started to tell them to fuck off, to get away from him, when he felt his mind being raped. They were running in his head like they were going to kill him, and he hurt from it. Someone told him to hang on, to keep helping them, but the pain was too much. As he let his hold on everything slip away, he heard someone screaming. Sterl hoped to Christ he wasn't hurting anyone else.

~~~

Elijah had been sitting with his brother for an hour when Sterl just sat up in bed. It had been five days since he'd been put in his room, and someone had been with him round the clock since then. He looked at him for a few seconds before he lay back on the bed.

"I think someone tried to kill me." Elijah laughed at his brother. "No, I'm not kidding. I feel like I've been run over several times, then laid out in the sun to bake. What the fuck happened?"

"Noah and Myra, who I might add is a very strange person, had to go into your head and take the bitch out. Not my words, but I'm pretty sure that it was apt. By the way, you stink too. Should you care." Sterl said he wasn't sure he could stand just yet. "Yeah, that's another thing. Noah had to give you a bit more of his blood. Joe too. They said that if you started to have fangs to let them know and they'll explain that to you."

Sterl sat up, and Elijah laughed. It was a joke, but Sterl didn't seem to find the humor in it. As he lay back down, this time on his side so they could look at each other, Elijah told the others that he was awake.

Is he okay? I mean, does he need anything? Elijah told their mom that he was weak but looked okay. He was building his strength to take a shower. *You tell him that we can come there now if he needs us. You take care of him.*

"Are they coming over? I'd rather they didn't right now." Elijah told Sterl that they would if he needed them. "Not right now. I just need to think. How long have I been out?"

"Five days. And it's mostly been rest, not recuperating. And so you know, I had to ask what the difference was. You were hurt by what they did, but you healed from that quickly with the blood of Noah and Joe. You've been sleeping—

resting, I guess — the bulk of it because your body needed it." Elijah helped him stand and held him while he stood there. "Alta, she's your cook now. She has been fussing around in your kitchen for days now. I think she wants to fatten you up."

"I don't really need a cook." Elijah thought for sure that he did. He had lost a great deal of weight. "Can you help me? I hate to ask you to help me shower, but I really don't think I can stand on my own."

It took them nearly an hour to get Sterl in and out of the shower. Twice Elijah thought he was going to have to call in some help as Sterl would just go weak on him. By the time he was dressed and sitting on the chair, Elijah felt like he'd run a marathon. But Sterl told him that he felt better, and he looked it as well. Getting him to the kitchen was much easier too.

When he ate what Elijah was sure was the first good meal he'd had in a while, Sterl decided after he was full that he wanted a nap. But after making him shift and run with him for a little while, he lay down by the pond that ran behind all of their properties and closed his eyes. Elijah asked him if he was all right.

Yes. I really think I am. I mean, I'm exhausted, but I feel like I could go to sleep now and not dream. I have been terrified of falling to sleep for a few years now. Elijah said nothing. He'd been there when they'd pulled that thing, a memory of her, and he wasn't sure that he'd sleep well for a while after seeing what Sterl had gone through. *I'm guessing that I'm in trouble. I remember hurting Trent.*

He is fine. I think you frightened us more than you hurt him. Elijah knew that Trent wanted to talk to Sterl right away, but Elijah asked him to wait a little while. *You had a part of her in your mind. She was there controlling you. Myra said it was a part of your brain that you use for emotions. She had attached herself to you so that you'd kill for her.*

I didn't feel her. Never. She never spoke to me either, so far as I.... She did when Myra held me. It was like her touch made it so I could hear her. Elijah knew that was exactly what had happened. *She's gone though, right? I mean, she's gone for good.*

Yes. Noah said that he felt badly for not checking your mind for her when he took her poison out of your body. Myra told him that he more than likely wouldn't have found her there, but Noah still feels like he let you down. And Joe has been by at least ten times a day to check on you for him. That bitch was there, in your head, to make you do things that would bring your beast out. Not the wolf in you, but something stronger. Something you don't have.

You mean the alpha. Elijah told him that was it. *She thinks I'm the alpha of our pack. That's why she fucked with me. Well, I got news for her, alpha or not, she has messed with the wrong person. I'm going to take care of her once and for all.*

We all are. We saw it too, what she did to you, and we're all going to take care of this bitch.

As they made their way back to Sterl's house, Elijah watched him carefully. He'd have to give a full report to everyone, and he was glad that Sterl was feeling better. By the time he left him, Sterl was having a snack, which looked like a one-pound steak and a pound side of grilled shrimp, before he headed back to bed. Noah was right about one thing; his brother was going to be better than ever.

CHAPTER 5

The check seemed to call to her several times a day, and Noelle would go and get it from the safe and just look at it. It wasn't the original check...that one was in the bank in a safety deposit box. This was a copy that she'd asked for. Even a copy of the check seemed to be surreal to her. Smiling as she put it back in the safe, she looked up when there was a knock at the door. Mr. Casen told her she had a phone call.

"But I don't know anyone that would be calling me." He asked her if she wanted him to tell them that she wasn't there. "I'm not sure. Who would it be?"

"I can ask for you, mistress. Perhaps you can come with me to the phone and I can give you some clues."

Nodding, she followed the big man out of the room to the kitchen where she thought the only wall phone was. Not just in the house, but the only one she'd ever seen. He picked up the phone and asked who was calling. She could hear shouting, but not really what was being said. Then Mr. Casen spoke again.

"I see. And Mr. Merrill, how is it that you got this number?" Noelle sat down on the chair and held tightly onto the table as Mr. Casen continued. "I'm not sure why anyone would share that information with you, but I would suggest that you lose this number and never call here again."

She could hear her stepfather then. "I know she's there. I want to talk to her. She's not been back to her place in a while now, and I heard that she was hanging out there. You tell her that it's time she got herself back to work and giving me what she owes me." Mr. Casen asked him what it was that he thought she owed him. "Money, damn it. She got me fired from my job and she owes me a lot of back wages. If she had just kept her mouth shut, I'd have been able to work and collect on some pension money too. She thinks I'm stupid."

"I'm reasonably sure that anyone that meets you can see that without being told." Noelle put her hand over her mouth when she felt a burble of laughter spill out. "Have you considered finding a job of your own? I mean, there are plenty out there. That way you can stop bothering the young lady who has done nothing to you, and have an income as well."

"I'm not going to dignify that with an answer." Mr. Casen just rolled his eyes. "What she doing there anyway? She working as a maid or something? Does that pay well? I could use me a few extra bucks this week, you tell her."

"No, she's not the maid." Howard asked what she was doing then. "None of your business. And should you call here again, I will have the number changed. Miss Noelle is no longer any of your concern."

When Mr. Casen hung up the phone, he stood there saying nothing. Noelle got up and pulled two glasses from the cabinet, found some chips, and shoved him into the chair. The man had done something for her that no one had before…stood up to her stepfather.

"He's a bully." Noelle agreed with him as she poured them both some tea. "Why on earth would someone just expect me to give them personal information like that? And to think that he thought you a maid here."

"He has every right to think I would be working as a domestic in a house like this. I'm not really from the kind of clique that Elijah and the rest of them hang out with." She ate several chips before she spoke again. "I missed how he said he got the number here. I mean, I'm guessing by now that he knows for sure that I'm here, but how did he get the number?"

"He claims that he got it from your previous employer. I shall have to look into that." She told him he might be telling the truth. Her old boss had wanted some way to contact her in the event that he needed someone to come and cover her shift. "You won't be working for him again. Will you?"

"No. But he thinks I will. I told him that I'd gotten a better paying job so he'd not question how I could suddenly afford to take off work." Mr. Casen got up and pulled down a big glass jar of cookies. "I can't eat that kind of thing, but you go ahead. Sugary things make me kind of loopy."

"How long?" She told him that she had no idea how long he was going to hope she'd come to work. "No, I mean how long has sugar made you loopy? All your life?"

"Yes. Howard did tell me once when I got all weird after having a slice of cake that my mom should have lived long enough to tell me about it. It was the one and only time that he ever said anything about her. I've never even seen a picture of her." She looked up at him when he continued to stare at her. "What is it?"

"Has Mr. Noah drank from you?" She shook her head and felt her fears tighten her back up. "Anyone other than Mr. Elijah?"

"No. What's going on? Why are you concerned about some sort of allergy that I have? It is an allergy, right? I have some sort of reaction to sugar." He shook his head and sat down. "You're really starting to scare me a little. What is it, Mr. Casen?"

"Witches need sugar to replenish their energy after they are spent. There are a few others too, other beings that need sugar to do the same thing. They drink fruit juices that make them feel better, eat a cookie or two, and can go about their business." She nodded, not wanting him to go on and needing him to at the same time. "Then there are beings that sweets affect them much like you are telling me. Children of vampires that have been born of a mortal human and an old and powerful vampire."

"You think I'm part vampire?" He nodded. "No. That can't be right. I have a normal mom. I never knew who my dad was, but my mom, she was as normal as I am."

Baby, are you all right? She nearly screamed when Elijah spoke to her. Mr. Casen asked her to tell him, to see what he said about it when she told him who was talking to her. *Are you in trouble? I can feel your fear.*

Mr. Casen thinks I'm part vampire. Or something like that. When he didn't speak, she continued, her fear overriding everything else. *He said that because I can't eat sugar, that I might be a child of a human and an old vampire. Why would it matter if the vampire is old or not? Not that I think this is true, but I was just wondering. I mean, had I been a vampire, wouldn't someone have told me?*

Old vampires, ones that were born to a pureblooded family, have powers that a great many people don't know about. One of them is that they can breed children with a human that is not their mate. Not all the time, but there have been occasions when it's happened. Does he have any idea how to figure it out? She told him what he'd said about Noah. *You should ask him. He might be able to tell you. Not that it matters to me, but it might change a few things for you if you ever want me to convert you to a wolf.*

Why? She wasn't sure that she wanted to know that either, but plowed on. *I mean, I've never thought of being what you are. A wolf, I mean. But I don't understand why whatever is in my background could change what happens, do you?*

Yes. It could change a great many things. The fact that Joe was a day walker for Noah and the powers that he gave her to keep her safe is one of the reasons that Trent hasn't changed her to a wolf. Not that it matters to either of them, but it might do something to the magic they both share. I'm thinking we should look into this. That way we won't run into trouble should it be true. She looked down at the cookies and decided that she was going to eat the entire container of them. But she knew that she'd be sick afterwards, not to mention it would make her feel as if she'd been on a three-day drunk. *It's going to be fine, love. I promise you. Whatever it turns out to be, it doesn't make me love you any less.*

I've never heard of this before. Is there a place where this is all written down? He told her that he had a book on their kind, but they usually depended on the others to help when something else come up. *So they keep things from you too?*

No, not usually, but I think the reason that this isn't public knowledge is because of the fallout from it. Can you imagine the problems that would arise for an otherwise normal person to have someone think that they might be a vampire's child? Simply because they don't care for sugar? I mean, every diabetic in the world would be persecuted, don't you think?

Yes, she could see that. Even if it was just a myth that had been going around, people would have taken it as gospel and there would have been a lot of people staked through the heart, much like women had been burned at the stake in Salem all those years ago. So it was decided that Noah would see if it was true or not. Noelle thought that she'd rather not know, but she could see the point in knowing as well.

~~~

Trent stretched, trying to loosen the tight muscles in his back after working on the walls in the building they were renovating. He didn't think they were ever going to get this place up and running at the rate they were going. He looked at his dad when he came in the room with him.

"I found a good place to put that desk you unearthed. Never saw one that big, did you?" Trent said he hadn't. "Anyway, I have some of the pack coming over to get it in the morning. I'm thinking that place over there on Fourth, the one that we decided to hold off on, it might make us a nice little second hand shop. What do you think? There is always people looking for something or another. Might have some fun with that."

"So long as I don't have to mess with it, I don't care." His dad nodded and helped him lift the next board into place. "Joe is going over to Elijah's house after she gets done working with Scott tonight to check on him. After that, she's coming here. Then I think she and I will head up to the cabin for the weekend. I need some time away."

"Good, that's good. I was gonna talk to you about that girl anyway. Noelle, do you think she might object to coming to work for me?" Trent asked his dad what he had in mind. "Well, I got that idea I was just telling you about. And I thought maybe I'd have her scouting around finding things to fill it with. Her and me with your mom, we could go on some hunting trips."

"And what is Elijah supposed to do while you're running all over town with his mate? I'm pretty sure that he's gonna want to be with her as much as he can. Even with him still working, I'm pretty sure that he doesn't want her gone when he comes home. Besides, right now it's not too safe for her to be out and about. Her stepfather hasn't been dealt with yet." His dad nodded but didn't say anything. "Dad, you already asked her, didn't you?"

"Well, it was a good idea, don't you think?" He nodded and had to smile. "Your mom, she was keen on it too. Spending time with a female is a lot more fun for her than hanging with you boys. Even I get tired of you six at times. I know you find that hard to believe, but sometimes I think you boys are just out to make fun of me."

"Whatever gave you that idea?" His dad looked at him. "Elijah will have to know where you're going all the time. And, like I said, just because he goes to work every day like he does doesn't mean that he wants you hanging out with his mate. He might think you're a bad influence."

"What a thing to say to your own father." Trent just laughed. "She's a little bit afraid of me, I think. Not me, just men in general. I blame that on her daddy. He's a real bastard. I can understand it and all about her being put off, but it still ain't nothing I like."

"I saw her stepfather the other day. He's a big man, did you know that?" His dad nodded. "He called the house today too. Earlier this morning. Elijah let me know, and then I called out there and Casen said that she'd taken it all right, but there is another issue that we have to look into." Trent told his dad what Casen had discovered.

"You think that she might be some old vamp's child?" Trent said that he had no idea. "Might be the best thing for her if she is. I know that she's like us now, with all that Joe and Noah juice running through us, but it won't hurt her to have a little extra. That man, Merrill, he might learn to back off if she were to come at him with a little of her own magic."

"It might not be anything." His dad nodded again, and Trent held up the next board while his dad shot screws into it. "Dad, what do you think of what we're doing here? This work that's going into this building? We might not get the project."

An investor was coming into town next week...well, he was one of four that were to come in. Trent had gone to see the city council at their last meeting and had asked to be put in charge of bringing new development to the town. Most of the people, pack included, were having a hard time of it with no jobs to speak of, and people were having a hard time making the few jobs that were there work. He and his family had money, a great deal of it, but they'd worked outside the town and had made their money that way. The ones that lived here, with no desire to travel like he had, were hurting.

"You said yourself that if we can't land us one of them contracts that the building will be put to good use. I was thinking that if they decide that we're too little for them — you know that's a good possibility — we can use this place for some of the downtrodden around town. And putting a little makeup on this old girl will make the city look a little better." The little makeup, as his dad had called it, had cost a great deal to get done. And they didn't even have anyone interested in it right now. "Who you got coming in next week anyway?"

"One of them is a producer for plastic ware. They make all sorts of things at their company, but when I talked to the buyer, he said that if they did come here, they'd be doing one of three things. I don't know what those might be, but that's what he said." Trent held up the final board for his dad to screw in place. "The other two are very hush hush about what they want the area for. I have an idea whatever it is, we're going to need a much bigger place than anything this town could handle. The plastics company said they'd hire five hundred people right off. The other two said they'd only need about twenty-five, as they were fully automated."

"We need the jobs more than we need automated." Trent agreed as the two of them gathered up their equipment. "Noelle and Joe are coming over soon. I forgot to tell you when I was talking to Noelle a bit ago. Joe said you knew, I guess. Noelle is a bit skittish and said she needs to talk to you about something. I told her we were working but could use a break, so to come on over."

Almost as if he'd conjured them, the two women showed up. Joe came to give him a hug and kiss and Noelle looked around. Dad was showing her all the work they'd done to make the building presentable.

"I worked for this man once that was point man for a company that made cereal. I don't think it was any good, the cereal I mean, but they thought they needed to expand." Trent asked her what the name of the company had been. "Good Eats. It was a terrible name, but he said they wouldn't change it."

"I remember them. They came to us, Elijah and I, when they were having trouble. We told them the same thing…that they needed to change their name to start with. I think they went under a few months later." She nodded and moved around the room, touching some of the things they'd found in the rooms when they'd started working. "What does this have to do with our building?"

"Oh. He would go to a place to see if it was a good spot, he told me. And while there, he said that he always looked for the same three things before he even sat down with the town. Cost, of course, but that could be worked through. But he said that there needed to be growth room. If they needed to expand, was there room? Could they expand their parking lot without a great deal of extra trouble? The second thing was a landing strip. There needed to be someplace close that a plane could be landed without a great deal of travel for the big bosses. He said for as much as they hated to travel to smaller towns, they didn't care to spend a great deal of time on the road to get there either." Trent thought they had both of those covered. His family had a strip that was used by smaller planes when necessary, and could be converted into something public if need be. "The third thing was an expressway. Trucks, if they're needed, should be able to get on and off the freeway easily and quickly. He said that the empty buildings, lack of paint, or new doors and windows weren't what he saw, but how the town looked as a place to live and work."

"There's a highway not ten miles from here. And the rest we have covered." When she continued to walk around, he asked her what else. "I think you have an idea, and I for one would like to have an edge when they get here."

"You don't have time to finish it, but I would suggest that you put in a couple of bed and breakfasts that cater to the people coming in. Mark said that he knew it was sort of silly, but he loved the Mayberry kind of mentality when he got to a town. One thing that he told me he enjoyed was when he'd walk down the main street and see the front windows of the grocery store painted with specials. And the local schools that way too. He said it told him that it was a town that came together when necessary." She turned to him then, her face red with embarrassment. "I don't know why I even mentioned it. I'm sure you know much better than I would."

"Doubtful any of us would have thought of windows being painted. But I can see the appeal of it." He looked at his dad. "You remember when we were little and Marshalls had his daughter put the big signs in his window to tell when chicks were in for the spring? And when there was salt in for the sidewalks?"

"I do. Sometimes I'd just go down there to see what she might have come up with." His dad was warming to the idea. "And you know Mrs. Baker, the one that lives down there on Wilson Street? She's been threatening for weeks now to open up her house to some people who needed a place to sleep. Why don't we give her house a nice little once over and have her run it for us?"

Trent's mind was running full steam ahead. The house could use a paint job, and he knew that her lawn needed to be mowed more often than she was able to take care of. It was on his list of things to bring up at the next pack meeting, that they should be caring better for the elderly. When he asked his dad about getting the place spruced up, he told him he had it covered. Trent looked at Noelle and smiled.

"I need you to come and work for me. For a few weeks anyway." She was shaking her head. "Not forever. But until we can get some growth in this town. You have a good head on your shoulders, and I have a feeling that you have a lot more ideas than you just suggested to us."

"I don't know what you want. I just told you what someone else told me." He nodded, already thinking of other ways she could help him. "You have that look in your eye. The one your mom has right before she suggests something that I'm probably not going to like."

"You'll love it. And on top of that, I'll owe you. These are ideas that are going to give us an edge we might not have had before. This town needs the business, and you helped me in that area." She narrowed her eyes at him. "Having the pack leader owe you something is a great thing. You will be the envy of everyone."

When Joe snorted, he turned to look at her. Before he could ask her what that meant, she stiffened by the window. Without a word, he looked over her shoulder and saw the three men walking down the sidewalk. Howard Merrill and his sons were out and about, and no doubt looking for trouble.

"Joe, why don't you and Noelle stay up here while I go and see what they might want?" She said that she could do that, but before he could tell Noelle that Howard was there, she looked out the window and saw for herself. "I'm going to have Elijah come here to be with you. I want you to wait here for him so that they can't hurt you."

"They might hurt you." He didn't tell Joe that there wasn't any way for them to do that, and said nothing when she put her hand on his arm. When she stood in front of him, he waited to see what she said.

"What do you want to do, Noelle? We'll support you in any way." Noelle looked up at him, and Joe said her name again. "He will as well. He might not like it. I'm pretty sure he won't, but he'll support you in it. Whatever you decide."

"They can't continue to run my life." Joe said that they thought they could. "I don't want them to think that. I don't even want them near me anymore. What right does he have treating me as if I'm his automatic bank? I have things I want to buy too."

"So you want to go and ask him that?"

Trent didn't think that was such a good idea, but didn't say it out loud. Instead, he reached for Elijah.

She needs to do this, I think. She has bad dreams thinking of all the ways that her father will hurt us or her again. I think if she could stand up to him, then she might feel better about herself. Trent asked him if she should do that alone. *Hell no. I'm nearly to her now. I'm coming in the back of the building. I'm just me for now, but I'm going to protect her with my wolf if I need to.*

Before he knew it, he was following his wife and sister-in-law down the stairs to where Elijah was just coming in the building. Trent thought that this was going to be epic, if no one was killed over it.

CHAPTER 6

Elijah wanted to stand in front of her, but knew that on some level if he did, she'd be afraid for the rest of her life. And according to Joe, that was going to be a very long time. So he stood beside her as she walked out of the building and into the path of her stepfamily. Howard drew back to slap her, and he nearly laughed when Noelle grabbed his arm and twisted it so that her stepfather ended up on his knees in front of her.

"What the hell are you doing? Let me go this minute before I have to beat your ass. Not that I won't anyway, but you are going to be hurting worse if you don't." Not only did Noelle continue to hold onto his arm, but she told him to shut the fuck up too. "You will not talk to me that way. And where is my money?"

"Unless you left money with me, which you didn't, then I don't have anything that belongs to you. Do you have a job?" Howard just looked at her, confusion written all over his face. "I asked you if you have a job. Do you? Because that's the only way you're going to get any money as far as I'm concerned."

"You owe me." Noelle said she owed him nothing. "You made me lose my job. What were you thinking when you told my boss that I'd just left you there? You got me in trouble with him."

"You *had* left me there, you moron. And I didn't tell him anything...you did that all on your own." He called her a liar. "No, when I asked to borrow Noah's phone to call you he heard us. You do remember that, don't you? When you left me, without a word, what was I supposed to do but to try and figure it out? But he let me use his phone, and then he listened in when you told me that you had no use for me other than my check each month. I think that is what you're talking about, right? How you think I lost your job for you?"

"You couldn't have went to anyone else to get a phone?" She said that she could have, but she went to him. "So see? You did that on purpose. You made me get fired, and now you're going to pay me for your stupidity."

"I'm not stupid anymore. I might have been before today, letting you take and take from me, hit me when it pleased you, but no more." When one of the other men with her stepfather moved, Elijah growled low and the kid stopped. "You move again, Ron, and I'll have him take your throat out."

The look on the kid's face was priceless. Elijah had a feeling that he knew just what he was, and was afraid that his stepsister would do just that. But the other one — Daniel, he thought his name was — wasn't that smart apparently. When he reached out his hand and grabbed Noelle, Elijah never got the chance to move. Joe hit him with something, and the kid hit the ground.

"What the fuck are you doing to my boys? You leave them alone, you hear me? They're all I have." Noelle looked at him, and Elijah knew in that moment that she had had enough of these bastards. "Get off me, you fucking bitch."

"I'm going to let you go, but if you ever come around me again, even to borrow a nickel, I will have you arrested. I'm finished with you." He stood up when she let him go and looked at him. Elijah wanted to knock the man into next week, but he waited. He knew just when Howard thought he'd sized him up and found him lacking. Howard drew back his fist, and Elijah spoke through his clenched teeth.

"You do it and I swear to you that you won't be as lucky as the last man who tried it." Elijah watched his bravery turn to fear. He popped his neck as Howard continued to stare at him.

"You think I'm afraid of a stupid mutt? I'm not. And you better bet that when I get you alone, I'm going to show you that I mean business." Elijah grabbed Howard around the throat and lifted him from the ground. He was a heavy bastard, but he let his wolf help. "Let me down."

"You touch my wife, and I will hunt you down and tear you into so many pieces that no one will ever know that you're dead. If anyone were to care." Howard looked at Noelle, then back at him. "Yes, my wife. You touch her or come near her, and that will be the last anyone ever hears from you again. Understand?" Elijah tossed him away from him and watched the man struggle to get up. Noah came to stand by Howard and put his foot on his chest.

"Hello, Howard. It's been a very long time, hasn't it?" Howard called him Mr. Stark and told him that he was glad to see him. "Too bad that I'm not all that thrilled to see you. You have been bothering some friends of mine. And for as much as I love them, I dislike you ten times that amount. Did you know that I've taken young Noelle and her husband under my wing? Well, the entire Calhoun family, really. And when you threaten one of them, then I have to assume that you're threatening me as well. I'm not one to fuck with, in the event that you might have forgotten that."

"Calhoun?" Elijah could see the dawning on his face. "You can't be married to her. She's nothing but a pizza jerk in some dump. They don't even make all that good of food either. Marrying her is beneath you, Mr. Calhoun. Christ, what is this world coming to when not even the rich are following the rules?"

"And what sort of rules are those?" Elijah looked at Trent when Howard didn't answer him right away. "You know something that we don't know?"

"Well, you should know that you should never marry beneath you. I did that once and look what it got me. Stuck with a stepdaughter that just wasn't like us." Elijah asked him what he meant. "Well, sir, she thinks that money should be saved up and not spent right away. I know that some think that's what you should do, save for a rainy day, but not us. We were stimulating the economy, and she was holding us back from that. Then there was the fact that she didn't want to come on the little outings that I put together for us."

"You were going to the company parking lot in the middle of the night and stealing things from people's cars." Noah said nothing but watched them when Noelle told them what he'd been doing. "And when you weren't doing that, you were selling off their computers and stereo's online that you'd stolen from them, and scamming those people as well by lying about sending shit out. So no, I wanted to not be a part of your little outings."

"You stole from the people you worked with? Why? Weren't you making good money working for me?" Howard only waved Noah's question off. "So this was a game for you? You just did it for fun?"

"Of course. It was a blast to see their hangdog faces when they realized they'd been hit. I tell you, I even sold a few of them back their shit at the next garage sale we had." Howard laughed. "Then after she got me fired, we had to do that for real. I really hated it when you put up the big fence around the parking lot. Sure did cut out my business. I don't think that was all that nice of you to do something like that to a man trying to make a living. I don't suppose you can tell me when you're gonna take that down, can you?"

No one said a word. The man had just confessed to theft, mail fraud, as well as child endangerment. He'd berated his former boss for trying to protect his employees, and even talked about making a profit on the things he'd stolen.

"No. I put it up to keep monsters like you from taking things that didn't belong to you." Howard nodded, but said that Noah was just like everyone else. "If by that you mean that I'm honest and want those around me to be so, then I thank you. You should have been in jail a long time ago."

"Yeah, that's not going to happen anytime soon. I have a family to support." Howard looked at him, then at Noelle. "You got you a rich husband now, sad as that makes me that he lowered himself to your level, but you can give me a little more now. I'll expect you to give me as much as you can, starting now."

He put out his hand, as if she was going to fill it for him. Instead of doing that, Noelle laughed. Hard and for a long time. Howard looked as if he might try to hit her, but Elijah took a step to him. When she seemed to have some control over her humor, she looked at Howard.

"You're not getting shit from me. I can't believe that I ever gave you anything, and didn't have you arrested for abuse." He snorted at her. "You think I can't? Well, the police are here now, so I think this is as good a time as any. Officer,

I'd like to press charges against this man. He's been beating me up and taking my money for years now. And he kicked me out when I was only sixteen. Also, he just confessed to stealing people's personal things from their cars and making a profit from it."

He was jerked from the ground and held above it. Elijah wondered how they were going to make the charges stick when Noah spoke to the officers. He was guiding the men, pure and simple, and Elijah was glad. Maybe they'd be safe for a little while longer with him locked up.

"Take him to jail. Charges are pending, and he has no use for a lawyer." Howard agreed with that. "Once he is there, he is to be treated fairly but without any kindness. If anyone asks questions, refer them to me."

Howard was still screaming about not paying for a damned lawyer, they were all crooks. That he hated them all. Then he turned to Noelle, and Elijah held her to him as Howard spewed his anger at her.

"You ain't nothing to me and you never were. Why I even bothered to keep you after your momma died is beyond me. I want nothing to do with you. Not ever." Elijah tightened his hands on her shoulders and held her. "You hear me? You are nothing to me and never was. I wish you'd have died when she did."

"Then you'll be happy to know that I want nothing to do with you either." As he was cuffed and taken away, his sons followed him like there was a leash on them that dragged them along with him. That man was the stupidest person he'd ever seen, and he wondered if the boys would ever amount to anything either. Turning her body to his, he held her as Howard was taken down the street with two cops on either side of him. "I should have told him I won that money. That would have made his day."

Elijah laughed with her. He told her that he was proud of her. Standing up to a bully was a good way to take control of her life. Then Trent started to laugh and they all looked at him.

"That turned out better than I thought it would. Very nicely too. I think this calls for a celebration." Everyone cheered, and Elijah felt like a great weight had been moved off his shoulders. "My treat. I've called the others in and they're on their way. We'll have a nice dinner, talk about anything but what just happened or is going to happen, and have fun. Even Sterl said he felt good enough to come in and join us. To me, that's the best news I've heard in a while."

As they made their way to the restaurant, Elijah held onto Noelle's hand. He knew that she was upset, he could almost taste it around her. But she was also feeling pretty good about herself. And to him that was the greatest thing ever. She'd stood up to her tormentor and came out on top. Also, he wondered if she realized that Howard had just confessed to not being in her life, something that was going to come and bite him in the ass when the check was made public.

~~~

"You go on back and tell that husband of hers to give you the bail money. There isn't any reason for him not to help out a man in need." Ron just stared at him. The boy had been doing that a lot lately, like he didn't want to be a part of whatever they were doing. "Do you hear me? I said to go and find Mr. Calhoun and tell him how sorry we are that he's married to Noelle, but he needs to get me out of jail."

"I don't think that's right, Dad. That man is married to Noelle, not to us." If he'd have been at home, he would have hit the boy. "I think we should just go out, find us some jobs, and then pay for our things the right way. I want to go to college, and I can't get a loan without a job."

"What do you want to go to college for? I didn't, and I had a good job until that bitch out there messed it up for me." Ron looked at Daniel and neither of them said anything. "What are you waiting for, an engraved invite? Go on out there and do as I told you."

"No. I don't think I want to. Not anymore. All this sneaking around and taking things that don't belong to us? I don't care for it anymore. I'm not sure I ever did." Ron started away and turned back to him. "You might want to figure you out a lawyer, Dad. I'm done with you. And so you know, I think that what you did to Noelle was wrong. All of it. I'm not going to be doing it anymore."

When he was gone, Howard looked at his oldest son. He knew that he had something on his mind, but Howard didn't have any use for touchy feelings right now. He told Daniel to go out and do what he'd told Ron to do. Like his brother, he was starting to get on Howard's nerves, acting like they got some sort of beef with him.

"I'll be dealing with him once I'm out of here. That girl, she owes me for what she did to me, and she's going to start paying up right now. No more screwing around with her dodging us either. She'll move back in with us and start taking care of us like she should have been doing all along now. I will admit I was wrong about kicking her out. We sure could have used us a housekeeper after your mom died. And I think I've been nice about her so far, and I'm not going to be now. She needs to know her place." Daniel said nothing. "Are you listening to me?"

"Yeah. But I have a question about some things. How is it you blame her for everything? When you lost your job, didn't you lose that because you just up and left her where she didn't belong? And I heard that you admitted to telling her that you only wanted her check; is that right?" Howard said so what. "And when Mr. Stark put that fence up around his property, you said it was because Noelle had told him to do it. That she'd convinced him to make our life harder. Now that I think on that, you never did tell me the real reason you stole all those things from them people. And I asked you too. And the one time you answered me, you said it was to get back at Noelle, but I think you just liked it. You know what? I don't even think she knew what was going on about that either. And the man who cut off our cable, she didn't do that, or a lot of other shit that you blamed on her."

"What's your point? I'm sure you think you might have one." Daniel nodded but continued to stare at him. "Well, when you get around to thinking one up, you tell me. But for now, I need for you to go and do as I told you. And don't think that I'll forget about this when I'm out either. I don't stand for backtalk."

"You don't stand for a lot of things when someone is questioning you, do you, Dad?" He didn't like this and told his son that. "Yeah, well I don't like being tossed around like we got done to us out there either. She handed us our asses, when I have a feeling that she could have had us killed and not thought another thing about it. And all you could do was see how she wronged us, when it was us all along that had been wronging those people. Hell Dad, we'll be lucky if you don't drag us all along with you to prison."

"There won't be anyone going to prison if you just do as you're told." When Daniel started for the doorway, Howard sat down on his bed. This was just stupid. He'd been wronged, and the sooner his boys saw that the faster they could get back to business. There was money to be had around here, and he was going to be just the man to make it.

Howard had seen a load of new construction stuff being delivered just today, and he was sure he could make a tidy profit off it, as well as anything else that might have come in. Then there was the large bulldozer that had been delivered just down the road from the construction stuff. Taking it might be difficult, but he was sure that he could get someone to buy it off him and get it out before anyone noticed. Howard wasn't without a few contacts.

It was perhaps an hour later when his dinner was brought to him. The tray had a salad on it, a small sandwich that looked like it had been smashed a bit before it had gotten to him, and a cola. There was an apple too, as well as an orange. He asked the man who had brought it to him when he was getting his real food.

"That's it for tonight. We didn't know you were coming, so had to get you something from the diner. And from the looks of you, I think you should watch a few things you put in your mouth anyway. You certainly don't watch what you spill out of it." Howard picked up the tray and was ready to toss it back at the cop when he laughed. "You do and you'll be pretty starved when breakfast comes in the morning. If you even get anything. I was thinking you should be more appreciative of what you have."

Howard might not throw it, but he wasn't going to eat it either. This was just cruel. He needed food, not this snack that wasn't even going to fill his belly for an hour. But the longer he sat there, nothing else came to him. No steak like he wanted, no fat potato with all the trimmings, and not even a piece of pie or two for dessert. He picked up the sandwich and examined it.

"Two pieces of bread and three slices of meat? What sort of meal is that supposed to be? Not even a big bag of chips or some peppers on the side for me to munch on." He bit into the sandwich and found that there wasn't even any mayo on it. Howard liked it thick on his sandwiches, along with about half a pound of cheese. Eating it, he tried to ignore the salad, but there was no hope for it. He was about to pass out, he was so hungry. Eating it without the diet dressing that they set on the side, he eyed the fruit like it was a bomb about to go off.

He couldn't remember the last time he'd eaten fruit that wasn't in a pie or on a slab of cake. Even then he'd work it to the side while he filled his belly on what he really wanted. And if there wasn't any ice cream or whipped topping to go on it, he'd get a bottle of syrup and pour it all over his dessert just to make it worth eating.

When the same cop came back to get the tray, he was just lucky that there were bars between them. The comments about how he'd done well with eating all his vegetables before his dessert was just too much. Treating him like a five-year-old was going to get the man seriously hurt. Howard had wanted to get up and beat the man to death with the empty tray and plastic plates. As it was, the fucker had laughed at him for ten minutes, standing in front of his cell while he did it. Howard asked him when his son was coming back.

"Back? I don't think anyone is coming to see you anymore. Ron said that you'd need yourself one of those court assigned attorneys, and Daniel said that he was leaving town and asked if that would be a problem. I told him that so long as he was gone for good, he didn't have to worry about the unpaid tickets."

Howard was still mulling over the fact that his own sons weren't going to help him out when he realized what he'd said. "What do you mean, he's leaving town? He can't do that. I'm sitting here in a cell and he can't just leave me here."

The cop said apparently he thought that he could. "You go get him and have him arrested. Put him in this cell with me so that I can teach him a lesson on respect and taking care of your parents when they need you."

"Respect? I'm pretty sure that we all thought that word wasn't in your vocabulary. But about those boys, I'm not going to do that. All of them deserves better than you." As he walked away, Howard wondered what the hell was wrong with people today. "You have yourself a nice night there, Howard. I'll be bringing you some light breakfast in the morning."

"Uppity is what they are. Just thinking on it, I can see them thinking that because Noelle got married to one of them Calhouns that they'd have to toe the line. And instead of doing that, they run off without me." Howard wondered what he was supposed to do until one of his sons came to their senses. "Stupid little shits. And after all I've done for them, too."

Howard hadn't been a good worker, even he would admit that. And he'd made himself much more important looking to his family than he really had been. There were days when he'd nap at his desk or play games online all day rather than do any actual work. But he'd figured, and still did, that if they weren't smart enough to know what he was doing, then it was their fault.

Then this thing with leaving Noelle at Mr. Stark's. He'd figured that she'd just run away, or worse, come on back to the house. He'd taken precautions about that too. Changed the locks, even had a gun by the door to shoot at her should she try to come in. He wasn't going to kill her, just scare her a bit. But she'd called him, something he'd not figured her being smart enough to do. He felt that the ordeal had been finished, that she'd known now that she was no longer welcome in his home. And had spent the weekend drunk and stealing shit for his kids for Christmas.

Then the next Monday, he'd gone to work, even cleaned himself up a bit, and was working on reading through the rules on a game he'd downloaded when Mr. Stark came into his little cubby hole and sat down. Howard had been singled out, he'd thought. Mr. Stark had come to see him.

"I met your daughter on Friday night. She's a lovely little thing, isn't she?" Howard had agreed and wondered what he was to do if he asked her for something. He had no idea where she'd landed her skinny ass. "You should know that kicking her out of your house is something that I don't condone."

"Kicking her out of the...what did she say to you?" Mr. Stark only sat there, and Howard tried to think what the stupid little shit might have said to his boss. "I'm telling you right now that she's not right in the head. She might be pretty and all, but she's not smart."

"Oh? Is that right?" Howard had nodded. "Well, that's too bad to hear. I thought she was very intelligent in her manner and words. And cooperative as well. She let me listen in on the phone conversation that she had with you after you abandoned her at my home."

"She did what?" Mr. Stark had only sat there, that weird grin on his face. "I was only teaching her a lesson on being nice to people. I don't think you might have heard it all."

"I dialed the phone for her. I was right there the entire conversation." Howard nodded, not sure how to salvage things. "As I said, I don't condone that sort of treatment to children. I hope you understand that."

"Yes sir. I do. And I'll make it up to her. I don't rightly know where she is. The stupid girl didn't even come home all weekend." He'd not thought of what she might have been doing at a single time all weekend. Only thought of her when he could almost see her face when she realized that she was on her own. "As soon as I find her, I'll make her understand that she can't be bothering you about this anymore."

"I would suggest that you leave her where she is. I have a feeling that she'd be better off without you and your family dragging her into your little schemes. Oh, and by the way, you're fired, Howard." Howard had stood up then, wanting to hit the man to have him take it back. "These men are here to help you out of my building and the property. You won't be able to get unemployment, so I'd not even bother with that either."

"I can't lose my job. I have a family to support. This is all her fault." Mr. Stark had walked away, and the security guards—three of them—told him to go with them. "I have to talk to him. He needs to see reason. She wasn't even my kid."

And now here he was, sitting in a jail cell for no good reason while his boys were out there all on their own, and that stupid girl, who had caused this entire thing, was living it up with a rich bastard.

CHAPTER 7

There was no hope for it. She was going to have to do this the old fashion way. Get to the wolf, have him fuck a human, and create her beasts that way. It would be long in coming, but she figured once she had the first one, she'd just have him breed with every female he could corner and that would move it right along. She closed the books she'd found in the lab without understanding a single word written there. Learning to read hadn't been something that she'd thought of until now.

The lab was ruined. Even getting things up and running again wasn't going to work. She had no one to run things for her. The two men that she'd brought here to work for her had told her that they couldn't do what she wanted.

"What do you mean you can't do it? Of course you can. You just mix my DNA with his cum and then we have a monster." The first guy had told her that they needed an egg. One of hers. "I don't have any eggs here. I told you that the power was off and all the eggs that we had here weren't even fit for an omelet, Basil told me. I'm not sure what you want with them anyway, but if it's that important, I can get you a few dozen of them."

"Not a chicken egg, you idiot. An egg from your body. You are a female, right? You do know your own reproductive system, right? Christ woman, we can't use chicken eggs for you to have a child by. Not even a chicken for that matter."

She might not have killed him had he not laughed. And for so long. It had taken her nearly a week to find this fool, and in two minutes, he was dead. Not that his death hadn't been fun, but it was over and she'd had to go and find another guy. The fucking bastards weren't as plentiful as she had thought they would be.

The second guy had told her the same thing. It wouldn't work. And when she'd asked him about the egg, he'd explained it to her. They needed an egg that was produced from her body for the child to grow in. Then they would put it back inside of her and she'd have a child.

"I don't have anything like that." He nodded. "No, I don't. I have nothing in me like a human has. Just magic. The rest of it was useless to me, so I removed it."

"You must have a heart. Everyone has a heart." She told him that the only heart she had in her was the one she'd eaten before going to get him. "I don't understand."

"I ate it. The last man who laughed at me, I killed him, then ate his heart. But this thing with the eggs, there is no other way to make it work?" She handed him the book she'd found in her ruined lab and noticed the horrid look on his face. Good, she thought. She loved the terror of others. "Basil, the other lab guy, he took notes. He said that he made sure that all his findings were right here."

The man had read over the book for several seconds and handed it back to her. "This won't help anyone. It's about you, and his tricking you into paying him to work on a lost cause. He goes on to say how stupid you are as well."

"Read it to me. Tell me what he said." The man took the book back and read three sentences before she snatched it back from him. "There is no way that he was lying to me. I got him everything that he needed. Everything."

"Well, apparently he was selling off some of that too. And so you know, he thought you were going to kill him. My favorite part is where he says that at one point he had you bring him eggs, and that you brought him ones from a chicken. He put them in the incubator and then took the chick home for his children. Are you really that stupid?"

This time her rage was consuming. Not just of the man in front of her but the buildings surrounding the one she'd set up. As she left the wreckage, the place blowing up different areas around it, she took the book and went to her home. It was the only place that calmed her when she was like this.

Helenia walked around her lair. There was so much stuff in the room, furniture that had taken her fancy, jewelry that she'd liked, and even a few things that she still had no idea why she'd bothered with it. But she couldn't part with it. Any of it. The things here calmed her.

Reaching out to her alpha, she wanted him to kill. She might not be able to see him do it, but she could feed off his rage for a few minutes. When nothing touched her, not any part of the alpha, she tried harder. There wasn't anything there. It was as if he'd been killed.

"No. I won't have that. I found him first." Going out into the night, she reached further, far beyond where she thought he'd be. When she found Noah she nearly moved on, but he spoke to her.

Helenia. Causing trouble, are you? I think that, on several occasions, you've been warned to behave. She told him to fuck off. *I think not. If you were the only thing...and I do mean thing…left on this earth, I would not touch you. I'd rather meet the sun.*

I can do that for you. I have the power of several suns. You just stay where you are and I'll come there to show you. You should have been dead long ago. Noah asked her why. *I heard from Dante that you turned me into the Board of Vampires. You do realize that they have no hold over me. I am not a vampire.*

No. You're much worse than that. She thanked him. *Don't thank me. It wasn't meant as a compliment. I think with what you're doing now, I'll be able to take care of you as I should have done decades ago.*

Always such a sore loser, Noah. What is it that you think I've done to you? And I should also point out that Dante is dead. The idiot should have known better than to try and take me in.

I know about the wolf. Helenia felt a finger of something, a feeling that she'd never felt before, touch her. *What do you think is going to happen to you when you come here to try and take him?*

There will be no trying, Noah. He belongs to me. I have marked him as such. And even if he did put up a fight, I only want one thing from him. And once I have it, I will be the most powerful being in the world. He laughed, and Helenia felt her temper explode in her head. *Noah, you aren't strong enough to take me on. You know this. I'm more powerful than you'll ever hope to be.*

Do you really think so, Helenia? I don't. I've been around longer than you. And even without the added years, I'm still much smarter than you. Stupid never wins. Haven't you learned that? She started to tell him that he was dead, that she was going to kill him, when he laughed and spoke again. *He is no longer yours. I have taken him.*

You can't do that. I took him. When he was there for the taking, I killed to have him all for myself. The alpha is mine. He said nothing, but his laughter rang in her head. *I'm coming for you both. Tell me what you've done with him. I swear to you, Noah, you have pissed off the wrong being.*

She felt his power roar through her head. Even as she fell to the ground, her nose started hemorrhaging something green and vile smelling. Nothing like this had ever happened to her before. Her ears rang loudly until she was sick from it. And as she lay there, she saw him in her mind.

He raped her head and memories. Took her thoughts and plans and ran over them. She knew when he found the night she'd found her alpha and had tried to kill him. Even when she'd had other wolves in her sights and what she'd done to them. Other dreams as well, things that she had accomplished. Even where she lived.

You really are a monster, aren't you? The worst kind too. You don't even kill for any kind of magic. But I will kill you for pleasure. I'm coming for you, Helenia. And when I get there, you will know a power beyond what you think you have. You are nothing. She tried to tell him to fuck off, to make him tremble in his shoes. *You are no threat to me and mine. I am the power that you seek.*

This time when he hit her mind, she curled into a ball. Her body changed from her façade to herself back and forth, over and over until she burned from it. Her flesh peeled away from her bones, wings were torn from her back. Bones broke in her arms, only to be repaired but mended in the wrong direction. Her fingers bent back toward her wrists, while her feet twisted around until she thought them to fall off. And through it all, Noah laughed, his voice in her head as if he planned to be a part of her.

Come to me, Helenia. Let me kill you on my own ground. She told him no, that she'd kill him first. *Even after this, you think it still possible? That you are stronger than me?*

I will kill you and take my alpha. He will give me my greatest creations as yet. He laughed again and told her where he was.

I'm coming. You'll rue the day that you took what was mine, Noah. See if you don't.

As will you. If you think you can come here to try and harm me, then come to me. Come here and let me kill you. His laughter faded, but the pain in her body was never-ending.

When she thought him gone, she sat up. She hurt and her body was ruined. Touching her fingers to her leg, she cried out at the pain and wondered what he'd done to her. But before she could get up and get herself to safety, he was there again. His power took her under.

CHAPTER 8

Noelle walked with the man who had come to inspect the area. Trent had set her up, plain and simple, by suddenly having to be out of town when the man arrived. When Gordon Winchester pulled out his notepad and began making notes, she thought about some of the things she'd talked to Mark about just yesterday.

"When he starts taking notes, that's a good sign. If he doesn't, then it's a lost deal. Don't speak to him first. Let him see the town through his own eyes, not yours." She tried to remember not to guide him toward any of the downtown shops either.

"Do you know how many people would be willing to start working?" She pulled out her own notes. "I'm to understand that the people here, they think this is a bad idea."

"Not that I'm aware of. And there are seven hundred people out of work right now or willing to transfer jobs. Everyone is helping out and ready to start working if this site is chosen. The high school is willing to set up a place for you to interview anyone you want." He nodded and made a note on his pad. It was difficult for her not to sell him the place, but she kept her mouth shut.

"What can you tell me about tax credits and abatements?" She had no idea. That wasn't part of her part in this. She told him that he'd have to make a plan for them to give him those sort of numbers. Then he'd have to see the county attorney. "Other towns have told me that I can have what I want. That they'd give it to my company for the jobs."

"I don't know anything about that. All I know is that if you want to make us an offer, or even to ask about potential buildings, then the town's attorney can sit you down and tell you what they have to offer. I'm just the point guy in this." He grinned and nodded. "I'm to tell you that the local bed and breakfast has your office set up for you. Mrs. Baker also said to tell you that she'll hold supper for you tonight, but can't do that all the time."

They moved down the main street then. Tanner was there, leaning against the office door that he'd been setting up for business. He was talking to Elijah, and they were laughing. She wanted to join them, to be anywhere but with this man. He was rude and a pain in the ass. When they were near them, she introduced Mr. Winchester to them both.

"Your wife is very hush-hush about why you think this town is what we're looking for. She won't even tell me how many people are willing to work here. I don't suppose you can shed some light on things." Tanner asked him what it was he thought they were looking for besides jobs. Noelle wanted to smack the man. She'd done no such thing, and she had answered his questions. "Well, I can see that the town is a little on the down side. There are a few empty buildings in the downtown area. Are you expecting our company to do anything about those?"

"I wasn't aware that any of this was the company's concern. I was under the assumption that you were looking at the site out of town, not what we have within the city limits." Tanner looked at Elijah, then at her before talking to Winchester again. "I can tell you that we have seven hundred acres of land for sale that are already zoned for business, with another four thousand for sale if it comes to that. There is an airport nearby that my family uses when we come or go out of town. A highway that is just a little out of the way, but close enough that anyone coming in here to put in a business won't have to have a long trip to get to it." Winchester was making notes. "Empty buildings? Yes, we have them. The town has been a little on the negative side for a few years, but we're hoping to bring it back up with the influx of jobs. Whether you plant yourself here or not, we're going to take care of them."

"There aren't a lot of places to eat or stay. What sort of accommodation do you have in the works for me should I want to live here? I mean, the houses are in pitiful shape. And don't think I didn't notice that every car on the streets is a little outdated too." Noelle laughed. "You think my questions are silly?"

"No. I think they're stupid. You don't care if we have a place for you to sleep. And what concern is it of yours how old the cars are? They're paid for, not that you need to know that. But that's not really what you're doing, is it? You're making small talk because you've already made your decision, haven't you?" When his face stiffened, she knew that she was right. "Why on earth did you come here if you knew you weren't going to consider us?"

"Trent." Noelle looked at Elijah, then back at Winchester, confused. "I was hoping he was going to be here. I wanted to see his face when I told him that we were going to go with the place out west. Not as many acres nor as many people that need a job. But I'd do just about anything to make that man look bad. As he's done to me."

"Why, you petty bastard." She walked away, and Elijah followed her. Tanner was still talking to the man, but she was finished. Reaching to Joe, something that she only just realized she could do, she let her know what was going on and asked if she had a direct number to the boss.

I just asked Trent about a man by the name of Winchester. He said that he'd gone to a site to see about the expansion that a company had wanted to do. But Winchester was there already telling the owners that there wasn't any need for it. That the economy was going to take a turn and the owner would be in the hole. Trent told them to expand, lent them the money to do so, and the company owner is now one of the richest people in the business world. I guess he also let it be known that this other shit told him not to do it.

I'm calling the man that hired him and letting him know. At this point, I don't even care if they build here. I just can't stand small-minded people.

Once she had the number, Tanner showed up in her little office. She told him what she was planning.

"Good. I might have a little talk with his boss too. This wasn't just a waste of time for us, but we could have been working with someone that didn't have a personal agenda." Noelle made notes as to what she wanted to say as Tanner continued. "Just be calm, honey. You can do this."

"If you get to talk to this guy, tell him about the money he's going to be spending on the extra electricity he's going to use to keep his employees cool all year round." Elijah explained to her what he meant. Making notes, she felt her anger fire up, but knew to lose her temper would make a bad name for them all. As soon as she was connected directly to the man, she told him who she was.

"I wanted to tell you what's going on with your man that you sent out here. Gordon Winchester is here looking at a site that you have picked for your new expansion." Mr. Coulier said that he knew that. He had been shown his notes. "Already? He's...never mind. He had already decided not to use our area before he got here because of a grudge he has for Trent Calhoun."

"Mr. Calhoun? I'm not sure what is going on, but I assure you that if he thought that.... Wait a minute. Calhoun? Are you based in Ohio? Trent Calhoun called my offices about two weeks ago. Mr. Winchester gave me the prospective on that place last week. Let me find it."

She told Tanner and Elijah what was going on. "The little pisser is playing us because Trent was a smarter man. How did he know what to tell him if he'd never been here?"

"That's what I'd like to know." She felt her face heat up when Mr. Coulier came back on the line.

"It says here that Trent had missed his appointment, and that after talking with a few of the townspeople, he learned that they were dead set against any kind of manufacturing plant coming to their town. And after further review, he discovered that the land that we were told about had several liens against it and that it was less than one hundred acres."

"We have never met with the man before he arrived today, Mr. Coulier." He told her to call him Doug. Noelle told him about the land and the people there. "Right now we have several hundred people who would like nothing better than to work. Few of them care what the job would be so long as it paid and they could catch up on mortgages. But I didn't call you to go behind his back. I wanted you to know what an unprofessional person he is. When he's out and about with your name on his lips, he represents you. And today, as far as I can see, he gave you a poor showing."

"And I agree. I wondered about this report, if you want to know the truth. It seemed as if it was a little one-sided, and sounded nothing at all like the reports I'd gotten from the people that had talked to Trent on the phone." Noelle told him that Trent was her brother-in-law and he was a good man. "High praise coming from you. Let me work something out. Can you hang on for a moment or two? How much longer is Winchester going to be there, do you know?"

"He's booked at Mrs. Baker's place for the night. I think we're taking him back to the airport at ten in the morning." He asked her again to hold on. She looked at the two men with her when she was put on hold. "I don't think he is very happy with Mr. Winchester."

"I should hope not." Elijah sat on her only chair and grinned at her. "I'm very proud of you for this. You have come a long way from the shy little mouse that I first met."

"You bring out the worst in me." He laughed, and she heard the line click. Tanner handed her a note. "Doug, I just heard from Trent, and he said if you'd like to call him, he can be where he has a signal in an hour. He and his wife have gone away for a few days. It's been sort of stressful around here of late."

"I can well imagine. I'd like to talk to Trent in person if he can manage it. I have a flight booked to be there in two hours. I'd very much appreciate it if you didn't let our Mr. Winchester know we're coming. I've made arrangements with his boss to come with me. Let's just say that he's not very thrilled about this call either." She told him she was sorry. "Don't be. As you pointed out, he's there on my behalf, and I won't have my good name attached to poor attitude. I have enough of that at home with three teenagers living with me."

After they made arrangements for him to be picked up, she told Tanner and Elijah what was going on. They were both whooping it up when she felt her belly turn. Putting her head between her knees, she tried to think what the hell had possessed her to do such a thing. She had more than likely just gotten this man fired from his job. She told Elijah when he asked if she was all right.

"No, you didn't get him fired. He did that all on his own when he came here with a chip on his shoulder. And just to give you a heads up, Trent said they're coming home too. He wants to be here for you."

"Me? Oh no, I'm done. When that man gets here, I'm going to be at our house thinking about this meeting thing I'm having with Noah. I don't think he's going to let me put it off again." Elijah said that he more than likely would hunt her down if she did. Noelle wasn't sure that she ever wanted to know if she was part vampire. "I'm just afraid. I don't want to know that something is wrong with me."

"Nothing will be wrong with you however it turns out. You are still my mate. We'll still be madly in love, and we'll have as much sex as we can until we kill each other." She let him hold her. "I love you, baby. And will forever."

"You might not after this thing is over." He assured her that he would. "I hope so. I'm going to need someone to hold me when I fall apart."

She was going to too. As they made their way out of her office, she wondered what this man was going to say to her when he found out that she'd made that call. Noelle could only hope that he'd not pull out a gun and shoot her.

~~~

Doug liked what he saw when they landed. People were milling about the small air strip, but not too many. There was room for growth here too, should they need it. As he and

Jerry West made their way to the waiting car, he wasn't really surprised to see a woman and man waiting for him. He knew the young woman had to be his savior. He could also see that she was as nervous as hell.

"Mr. Coulier, this is my brother-in-law, Trent. My husband is here as well, but is just inside talking to his secretary since it was too noisy out here." Doug introduced them to Jerry and shook both their hands. Then he did the same to Elijah and TJ, their father, when they joined them. "We wanted to make a good first impression. I'm not sure what we're going to impress you with. I only wanted you to know about Gordon."

"As well you should have. He doesn't know that we're here, does he?" She assured him that he didn't, that he'd not left his room since he'd gone back there earlier. Jerry huffed. "Jerry is going to do this site analysis for me. He started this business from the ground up. And so you know, Gordon is his son-in-law."

"Never cared much for him anyway. But had to do something when I was paying for every little thing they needed. At least this way...well, I thought I was getting an honest return on my money. Apparently not." Jerry had told him that he'd had other complaints about Gordon, and this was going to be fun for him. But he was also making the young woman nervous. "You did us a great service here, young lady. I can't thank you enough."

When her face turned red, he looked at her husband. It surprised him at the love he could see on his face when he looked at Noelle. The man was absolutely besotted with his wife. As they made their way into the long limo, Elijah started filling him in on the details that had not been in the report that he'd been given.

"We're headed to the land site now. As Noelle mentioned, there are four thousand acres that we were looking at, and an additional seven hundred that are already zoned for business. The land hasn't been developed, but there is a site building on the first plot of land. A few decades ago someone came in with the bright idea to build homes out there. Not that it wouldn't have worked. The site is perfect for it, but all the developer got finished was the site building. It still has power, water, and gas." Elijah handed him a file. "There are the proposed tax abatements that we've talked over with the county commissioner. The mayor would have liked to have been there today, but his wife went into labor about an hour ago, and she said she'd kill him if he left her. It's their first child."

Doug looked over the paperwork, impressed that they'd been able to put this together on such short notice. "The plant that I have in mind for here would need at the very least two hundred-fifty people to start with. Then more as we gear up. Of course, we'd need to have a training crew come in to help them out. Would there be accommodations for them to stay as well?"

"Baker Bed and Breakfast can hold ten. She's a widower that had ten children, so it won't be a hardship on her. Also, TJ is renovating two of the buildings in the downtown area for apartments. Short-term ones for the present." Noelle pointed out one of the buildings as they drove down the main street. "The larger building will hold, I think he said twenty-two, the smaller building only about six. The space is larger there for families should someone bring them."

"I thought maybe, when you're all done with the comings and goings for this place, I'd turn it into a homeless place. Not a shelter, but a place they can come and get a shower, pick up a few items that they need. It's also gonna be a place where we can get them some training, like on computers and such. Get them back into society." Doug loved that idea and made a mental note to see about getting some of his people there to train them for the lines at his plant too. TJ continued, and Doug could hear the pride in his voice when he spoke of his sons. "Trent, he's got a buddy that has one of them tour bus businesses. He's going to rent us a few of them to get some of the people back and forth to the plant should they need it. A lot of these people have been out of work for some time, and a car isn't something that they've had for a time. Scott has donated some computers that his company is no longer using for them to use for resumes and such. Randle is a teacher, and he's been talking about an after school program for the kids of the families that get to work. If you move here."

As soon as the limo stopped and they got out and they were standing in the open field, Doug came to a decision. Really, it had been made when he spoke to Noelle, but seeing the land and the potential, he knew this was perfect. As he made his way around, looking at what he wanted done, he talked to Noelle.

"What can you tell me about the Calhoun family that I might not have already figured out?" She looked back at them, and he realized that they were allowing her to sell them. "You made this deal for them. I'd like to know the family."

"They're the best that I've ever been around. They pick you up, dust you off when you fall, but they don't push you into anything. TJ and his wife, Christine, they did well raising them up, making them into men that they could be proud of." He smiled when she got a sappy smile on her face. "I'm in love with their son, but the entire family has taken me into their hearts, and I like it there. That's probably not what you're asking me, but that's what I feel. And Trent does want this for his community. He's a good man, a better leader, and a pack master like none other." She looked up at him then.

"You know what I am." She nodded. "I've known that the others were aware that I'm a cat. Even Jerry is. But you're human. I wasn't sure how you felt about that."

"I don't care what you are so long as you're honest and trustworthy." She stopped walking, and so did he. When he looked at her, he could see something that he'd not before. Determination. "You hurt them or this town, and I will make it my life's work to make you regret it. I'm not threatening you into bringing your plant here. I think with what we have to offer, people will come anyway. But I'm talking about them personally. I love them and I won't see them hurt because I got my panties in a twist about someone that works for you."

Doug laughed. It had been a long time since he'd been impressed with someone that he was working with. Especially one that had put him so nicely in his place. And not only did he want to work with her, he wanted her to come and work for him. She was smart, loyal, and she told it like it was. Something few did when it came to him.

As they made their way back to the others, he knew that this was the site that he'd use. It wouldn't have mattered to him if some other place was giving him the land. This was where there was going to be heart. And that was what he'd strived for since he'd opened his first plant thirty years ago.

"My wife just contacted me. She said that I'm to bring you back to our place for dinner. It's family night, and she said that she's not going to miss it because we have company." He nodded at TJ. "Mr. West, you're more than welcome too. In fact, she insisted on it. And so you know, she's not one to turn down. My wife can be a tad on the fussy side when she makes plans and someone messes with her."

"I'd be honored. And I've been thinking about my boy, Gordon, too. I'm going to let him stew a bit, think he's pulled one over on me. Then tomorrow when he's to go to the airport, I'm going to be the one taking him. It's the very least I can do since he's done with my company." He put his hand out to Noelle. "I want to personally thank you for what you did for me. Like Doug here, I have a name that I'd like to keep untarnished. This was a black spot on my company for some time now. And I don't want you feeling badly because I'm going to fire him. He did that all on his own when he lied to me."

"He pissed me off, if you want to know the truth. I had been walking around with him for two hours, and all he did was dig at everything I said." Doug wanted to hug her. She was the freshest thing he'd seen in business dealings. "If you guys go someplace else, that's fine, but I won't have someone thinking we're not what we are, hardworking people with only the best in mind for the people here."

Doug asked questions about the town as they rode back to the Calhoun home. He found out a great deal about the family, the area, and their plans for it when things were settled about a plant. No one asked him if he was moving here. It was assumed, he thought, that he wasn't. Doug decided that he liked this family more with every minute he spent with them. And when he pulled up in front of the family home, he could only stare at the house and grounds.

The house was a three story mammoth of a place. Tall white columns held up second and third floor porches. There were rockers, pots of geraniums at each window, and pretty flowers at the railing all the way around. He'd bet anything that there was a pool in the back, as well as a kitchen garden.

The place looked like something straight out of the movies. Then Mrs. Calhoun came out of the house, and he smiled. Christ, she looked like a tiny and younger version of his own mother. Only this one would hurt him if he got out of line. His mom spoiled him.

"Mrs. Calhoun." She took his hand after hugging her sons and husband. "I wanted to thank you for inviting us to dinner. I hope that we're not intruding."

"Nonsense. Had I not wanted you here, I would have said so. We're having steaks on the grill tonight, and some sort of side that I don't know what it's about. And apple pie with homemade ice cream. Come along now. Meggie makes the most amazing pies this side of the country. And Joe is gonna whip up some of her biscuits." As they followed her into the house, she mentioned they had company. "I don't know what you feel about vampires, Doug, but you make a butt of yourself and I'll have to kick yours."

Doug paused on the step. Not that he cared about the vampire, but what she'd said. It was as no-nonsense as he'd come to realize that the entire family did things. Christ, he loved this family. They were all about as honest as it came. As he made his way into the house, Jerry pulled him aside.

"If you don't put your plant here, you're a fool. And you should hire that girl to work it in some way. She's got a hell of a head on her shoulders. If you don't, then I'm gonna. Christ, she'd be running my business in a week if I don't miss my bet. And I'd let her. She's that good." He told Jerry he'd already been thinking on it. "Good. I don't think you'd do any better if they paid you to be here, either. This place has it all. Including a family you can work with."

Doug didn't think he would find a better place either. And now all he had to do was convince Noelle that she needed him as much as he did her. He might even bring his kids here and let the Calhoun elders whip them into shape. Do them some good too.

CHAPTER 9

Helenia was sure that she'd never hurt this badly, and felt as if every time she moved, she'd find another place that hurt. Noah was going to pay for this. He'd hurt her and no one got away with that. Not and lived to talk about it.

She could no longer hold her other form. Going out in the daylight didn't burn her as it did a vampire, but it did weaken her. The sun could help her when she needed a little extra power, but right now it felt like it was cooking her flesh. Holding to the shadows, she tried to keep an eye out for any fool that was looking for her.

When she'd returned to her lair last night to rest and to recuperate, ten men had been there waiting for her. The Board had found her place of rest. She watched them from a distance, trying to decide if she could have taken them all, when she smelled it. Olive oil. They were killing all chances of her ever being able to stay in her lair again.

Olive oil, unknown to most anyone that hunted vampires, and herself included, would kill them. Not just the oils from the nasty fruit, but also the fruit itself. Just one touch to one of them would burn through their flesh to the bone, and then make it so fragile that it would no longer support them. Helenia could not believe that they'd do this to her.

As she watched, her anger getting stronger by the minute, she saw the flame just before it was tossed at her home. It was old and made of wood, so it went up quickly. The red flames ate at the only resting place she'd ever known. The only one that she could ever use.

Helenia wondered if Noah had seen where she lived in her mind and had sent them here to do this to her, knowing, as few did, that without her stone and her soil to replenish her, she'd begin to lose her power. Like the lore of vampires, she did need her home soil to survive. And the large stone she'd been put upon when born.

Helenia thought of how she'd come to be, how her power had come to her, and what rituals had been done to make her as powerful as any other being in the world. Few knew what it had taken to make her what she was, and those were long since dust in the ground. Killing them had been her greatest triumph.

Her mother had been a witch of the darkest path, her father a vampire that had long ago turned rogue. They created her, a babe, and had taken her to the sacrificial altar that they'd fucked on to make her. Even as her body, still damp from her birth, cooled her, they were pulling out the things needed to make her what she was today.

After summoning the demon from the other world, he blessed their blade and what they were about to do. He'd only asked for one thing...their own souls in return for helping them with their child. Then he looked at her, and Helenia knew him for what he was, and what he was going to do for her.

"You will be strong, my child. Your magic as powerful as I can give you. Once you are matured, your body no

longer of this earth, I will come to you and give you it all."
Even as a babe newly born, she knew his words and what
they would do for her. "I will help them with this, but you
will owe me still. A boon that I will collect when you have
been destroyed."

She wanted to tell him that she would never be killed,
that destroying her would be impossible. But he moved
away, and Helenia had felt calmed by the things that were
coming.

The blade was taken by him to finish what her parents
had started. He dipped it in his own blood before it was
plunged into her heart; the power of it, of his blood and
magic, gave her small body so much. Helenia hadn't
screamed, her body accepting of what was to come. And
when the blade was pulled from her chest, the blood that had
sustained her all those months in her mother's womb
covered the stone she had been on until it was stained with
it.

The screams of her parents had sounded like music to
her ears. Helenia was sure that they had thought they would
be around for a long time, that they would see their creation
run the world. But he took them both, killed them, then sent
them to hell to serve him. Helenia smiled at the demon when
he picked her up from the stone and laid her upon the soil at
his feet.

"The ground here will accept you like no one ever will
again, save me." She felt it covering her, the soil as hot as the
breath of the demon. "When you are mature, your body
ready to come forth, I will brand you as my own and you will
be free to do as you please for a period of ten thousand years.
After that time, I will come for you, if you are not harmed by
anyone in any way."

Just as the soil was at her neck, the heat of it burning at the flesh she'd been born with and replacing it with something more, he leaned to her once again and spoke. Helenia had forgotten the words he'd said to her until she'd woken after Noah had hurt her.

"A man will come to you. If he should wound you first, then you are finished. Your powers will go to all that surround you and you will wither and be gone if I am not there to take you. You will not die, for you are no longer living. And the power that you have now, it will no longer be yours. Do you understand me, Helenia, my child?" She had no way of answering him, but he seemed to understand that she had said yes. "If you allow this to happen, for this man to harm you, then I will expect you to be my slave, a slave like none other for the rest of eternity and beyond. Do you take this deal?"

Again, she had no way of answering him verbally, but he nodded once and stood. The darkness took her then. The soil cradled her into its depths for one hundred and one years. And when she rose up, her body as it was now, he came to her. The magic that he gifted to her was nothing compared to what she had gained as the years went by, but it had been a good start.

Now not only was she now without her home and her place of rest, but her plans to take over the entire world were put on hold. Moving closer to the buildings that held the most heat, for her body was freezing all the time now, she thought of what she was going to do to Noah when she found him. And find him she would.

Have they found you as yet, Helenia? The Board was most happy that I was able to give them specific directions on not just where to find you, but how to destroy your lair as well. Noah's voice made her pause. But it was his laughter that made her anger spiral out of control again. *I would like to tell you about the man that you thought to take as your own. He is safe from you. You will never take from him what you planned.*

You think not? Well, I have marked him first, and as such, he is mine. She laughed when he said nothing. *Can you see what I did to him, Noah? The dreams that I have given him so that he'd be weak when I took him? The way that I tainted his blood? When he is hurt, does he not heal as he should? I have heard that he has no will to have a child. I will have many by him, monsters as I am. They will do my bidding and eat the one that sired them for his blood.*

The last time I saw him, which was only a few hours ago, he was hale and hearty. His mind cleared of your dreams and his body as whole as mine. I wonder now if you are as strong as you think you are. I mean, the man has nothing at all wrong with him. Helenia didn't believe him and said as much. *You can or not, I don't care. But I do have to ask when you're coming here. You are, aren't you, Helenia? Oh, I so hope so. When you do, you had better be ready. Oh, I just realized that you won't be as strong as you might have been. Taking that information from you was very helpful.*

You think you hurt me by burning my things? I have many houses with many things in them that I care nothing for. She was sure he didn't hear her fear. But when he laughed again, she felt her temper take hold of her. *Noah, when I find you I'm going to enjoy killing you. And when I do, I want you to know that I will take my beast with me to my bed and let him create many children with me.*

He knows what you are. He also knows that you cannot create anything with him, not even so much as a selfie. You cannot bear a child any more than I can. She had no idea what a selfie was, but decided that she'd make him create one with her just to prove Noah wrong. *I will enjoy watching him destroy you.*

She refused to talk to him any longer. Her temper drained her, and she couldn't afford to lose any more of her strength sparring with a fool. When he laughed again, telling her where to find him, Helenia used some of her magic and turned herself to air and moved along the current to him. Noah was going to die, and she was going to kill him. It was all she could think about as she was tossed along the air like a bobber in water.

~~~

Elijah was worried. Not about what the small test results gave them, but how she was going to react to them. Noelle was afraid that they'd all shun her or turn her out. And no matter what he said to her, she steadily believed that they would. Myra came into the room just as they were all seated around the big living room. Doug and Jack had left for their hotel not an hour ago.

He was sure that Myra found the most hideous colors and smashed them together into some sort of dress. Tonight she was covered from head to toe in the most brilliant shade of purple he'd ever seen. It was almost neon, but not. Her hair, also purple, hurt the eyes when she moved, and looked as if it had a life of its own. When she winked at him, he was almost afraid to ask her.

"I understand that congratulations are in order." It took his mind a moment to catch up to what she was saying. While he'd been watching her, her color palate changed from the purple to a green just as blinding. "The plant will be here. It will give the area a much needed boost. So you know, my cat friends, the Bentley men, said to tell you that should you need any help they'd be more than happy to do so. I have told them all about my new friends, the wolves. Micah Bentley, he's the leader of their leap. He was most pleased that you are doing so well."

"Tell him that I'll keep that in mind." Myra nodded at Trent and sat down. "We were just talking about this test and what it might tell us."

"It will tell you wondrous things, I think." She looked at him again. "Elijah, are you taking the job working with Mr. West? I'm to understand that you won't even have to relocate, that you and Noelle can work for him from here."

"We have to talk about it together first. We're not sure. I have a job that I love, and Trent needs Noelle here to help with this plant and things with it. For now, we're working on this thing with Sterl and Helenia." Myra nodded, and they all looked at Noah when he appeared in the room. "We're ready when you are, Noah."

"Now, as I have said before, this will not only tell me if you are the child of a vampire, but if I know him, I might be able to tell you who he is as well. At the very least, I'll be able to know if he has passed on or not." Noelle nodded and held Elijah's hand tightly in hers. "I promise you, this will not hurt at all."

"Before you do this, I want to thank you." Noah asked her for what. "This thing with my stepfamily. Had you not helped me that day, there is no telling what might have happened to me should he have left me by the side of the road. You saved my life, I think."

"I think you would have done well no matter what else might have happened that day. You're brave and very smart. And today you were begged by not one but three men to work for them. I knew the moment I met you that you were something special." Noah looked at Elijah as he continued. "I don't have to tell you what a precious thing you have here with her. You will take care of her as she deserves, I know this. I'm very proud of you, Elijah."

"Thank you."

When Noah pulled her wrist to his mouth, Noelle dug her nails into Elijah's hand so tightly that he felt the trickle of blood as it raced over his hand. And when Noah lifted his head and leaned back, it was all he could do not to pull his hand from Noelle's and shake off the pain of it. His dad laughed and patted him on the back.

"You are the child of Roman Gallegos. Roman was a great and powerful vampire, and a man that I called friend. He is, sadly, passed from this world." Elijah let out a breath he'd been holding. "I do not believe that he knew of you. If he had, I think he might not have met the sun like he did. He was, like a lot of us when we get older, bored with his life, and ended it rather than turn rogue."

"So I'm part vampire." Noah nodded and smiled. "I guess my next question to you is, what happens to me now? I mean, can I be changed into a wolf like the rest of the family?"

"I'm not the one that can answer that." He looked at Myra, who smiled at them all. "She's been looking into a few things for me. In addition to Helenia, she had a lot of information about this sort of thing as well."

"Yes, there is no reason that either of you, Joe or you, cannot be converted. However, that being said, I would think on this for a little while. First of all, Joe would be able to be a wolf, but with the power that she received from Noah, she would also be able to shift into other animals as well. And so would Trent. As the alpha, that could be a good thing so long as the pack doesn't care." When she looked at them, he knew whatever she said to them wasn't going to be as easy. "Roman and I were friends as well. He was a kind and generous man, and if he lay with your mother, then he did so out of love, not as a one-night stand. They more than likely came together at a time in his life when he was low and her otherwise committed. He would not have taken her from her life if she had a husband. He ended his life not long after you were conceived. I would imagine, as Noah has said, had he known about you, he would have lived."

Myra stood up and came to them, her dress black now, as was her hair. Elijah wondered briefly if her moods, and not only her magic, changed her clothing. When she handed an envelope to Noelle, he looked at the logo on the front. The Board of Vampires.

"When he passed away, his things were put into a trust. The money, as with the other items that he left behind, were set aside in the event that someone, a child, came forth to file a claim against it. The money would be kept for a period of two hundred years. Then at the end, the money would be put in a vault with his name on it and be used should the need ever arise. I have talked to the Board and they have asked me to give this to you." Noelle looked at Elijah before putting her hands behind her back. "You must take it, child. Your father would have wanted you to have it."

"But I don't want it." She looked at Elijah again, and he waited for her. Whatever was in the envelope was hers, and he wanted her to have it. But if she didn't, then that was fine with him as well. "It should go to some sort of fund for someone that needs it."

"You can do that should you want to." The envelope was suddenly in her hands. "There. Now that that's settled, let us move on to Helenia."

"She's on her way here. I had a conversation with her just before things started to come together for your family." Noah got up and handed each of them a sheet of paper. "I had Joe make a list of the things that I found in her mind. There was a great deal to sort through, but this is the most important thing. The conversation she had with a demon just before she was turned is what is going to end this for her. And for you, Sterling. And so you know, this is the only creation of a she-devil that I have ever known."

"This man, this is you?" Noah shook his head at Sterl. "Then who is this person that is going to take care of her? I'm assuming that it must be someone powerful."

"He is. Very much so. I don't think he believes himself to be, but he is the only one that can take her down." Elijah got it right away, but Sterl took a bit longer. And when he stood up, the paper falling from his fingers, Elijah felt his wolf moving along his skin.

"No. And I can't say this enough, no fucking way no." Sterl looked at their mother. "I'm sorry, Mom, but I want him to understand that I can't do this."

"And why not?" Everyone turned to Scott when he asked. "Why do you think that you're not strong enough to take this woman out? She already thinks you're an alpha. And so you know, you are. You might not be as strong as Trent is, but I think that the only reason you aren't is because you've never tried to be. I not only think you can do this, but I think you should be the one to end her life."

"I can't do it." His dad stood up when Sterl started pacing. "I'm just getting my strength back from the last time she came at me. And that was almost five years ago. If you think I can do this, then you might as well have left me broken as I was before."

"You were never broken, son. You were down, but not out. That woman, she hurt you in more ways than we can ever know, I understand that, but there isn't any reason why you can't get her out of our lives."

"Dad, you have no idea what kind of things she did to me." He said that he did. "No, you can't know. You don't know the horror I felt whenever I thought of her. Whenever

I closed my eyes at night." His dad nodded. "She took everything I was from me."

"Only if you let her, son. And we did know the horror she put you through. We saw it in your face and eyes every time we looked at you. When we saw the way you hid from us, keeping away so that you'd think we'd not notice. You're our son, our family. We hurt when you did. We ached with you. Son, we were hurt because there was little to nothing we could do to help you. But we can now."

"I don't want to do this." Noelle stood up and said she would then. "You can't do this. You're mostly human. She'd kill you right away."

"I'll be beside her." Joe stood up then and held onto Noelle's hand. "I'll be there with her when she takes her on."

Elijah stood and took Noelle's hand into his. "I will as well. I give you both what I am and what I have to help."

Scott winked at him as he took his other hand, claiming that he'd be beside them as well. Each of them stood, giving their strength to Noelle. When she moved toward Sterl, Elijah wondered what she'd say to him. When he backed from her, Noelle took him into her arms and held him.

"I love you, Sterl. You're like the annoying brother that I always wanted. But if you don't want to do this, we'll do it for you. We'd gladly do this for you. But honestly, and I think you'll agree, you'll feel a hell of a lot better if you do this, take her on." He held her and sobbed that he was afraid. "So am I. Every day I get up, I'm terrified that my family is going to come for me. That once they find out about the money, then they'll beat me until I'm dead to take it. But you've been there for me. Every step of the way, you and the others have been there for me. This she-bitch? She doesn't stand a chance with all of us behind you."

"What if she hurts one of you? Then what will I do?" Noelle looked up at Sterl and grinned. "I don't think I like that look on you. It's sort of scary."

"If she hurts one of us, then we whoop her ass, but good. But you only have to hurt her, Sterl. There is nothing that says you have to kill her." Elijah looked down at the paper that was given to him and saw the words there he'd not thought of before now. "The demon only says that a man will cut her first, and then she will be finished."

"I don't understand. I only have to cut her and she's dead?" Elijah looked at Noah when he cleared his throat. "Please tell me that it's not that simple."

"It isn't and it is. You must cut her before she does you. And I assure you that she'll be trying her best to cut you as well. But the good news is, when she cuts you, you're dead. If you manage to cut her first, she becomes the plaything for a demon for the rest of eternity and beyond." Noah smiled at him as he continued. "I've been working with the Grand Witch and Myra. We have a way to weaken her even more than she already is. Helenia won't know what hit her until it's too late."

"Well, that makes me think this is going to be a walk in the park then. Just cut a woman who tears people in half for fun. Oh, and let's not forget that she can also levitate, as well as has these freaky powers that make her pretty much invincible to most anything I can dish out to her." His mom patted him on the cheek before she slapped him. "What was that for?"

"You want to live? Or do you want to sit around sulking about what she did to you?" Sterl told her that he wanted to live. "And how do you expect that to happen if you whine and moan about how you can't do this or that? Huh? Do you think this woman is just going to stay away because poor

Sterling doesn't think he has it in him to win? You think she's going to say, 'Oh well, let me go easier on the poor man, he's being such a baby.'"

"I'm not being a baby." Elijah laughed and his mom turned to him. When she seemed satisfied that he wasn't going to laugh again, she looked back at his brother. "She's a she-devil, not anything that we've encountered before."

"She's a woman after one of my pups. Do you think that she's ever come across anyone like me before?" Sterl shook his head. "You're damned right she's not. And don't you think I'm going to let you stand up to her alone either. She hurt you, and in my opinion, she's going to pay with her life. And you're going to do it. Now, I'm going to go and see if there is any pie left from dinner and have myself a piece. I, for one, could use a little treat."

When she left the room, Noah turned to him. "Remind me to never piss your mother off. I'm pretty sure if she were to run the Board of Vampires, we'd have no more problems like we have with Helenia."

"I'm pretty sure that if she ran the country that there be no more wars or fighting. She'd have some heads roll if there was." Noah nodded. "But you gotta love her. She's got Sterl thinking he can do this now."

"I know that he can."

Elijah hoped so. There was a lot riding on this.

CHAPTER 10

Elijah waited until the count of ten before he took off to the woods after her. Noelle had made him promise three times that he'd give her this head start. He'd had to start over twice when he lost track of where he was every time she sent an image of what she wanted him to do to her when he caught her. Christ, the woman was going to kill him.

He could smell her. Not well, but enough that he could find her. She told him that she'd been working on her skills in hiding. He was pretty sure that Joe had been helping her. And he knew that Joe had been teaching her a few other things as well. Like how to fight.

Hand-to-hand combat was something that his brothers thought that every woman should know. And once Joe started training a few of the woman in the pack on how to defend themselves, it had been a big hit within their group. Not that any mate could hurt their other half, but it was nice to know that they could protect themselves in the world around them. Especially now that the plant was going to bring in all kinds of people.

I don't think you're trying very hard. He wasn't and told her that. *Why not? Don't you want to play?*

123

I do. With you, but I was thinking about things. Mostly the pack, but also you. She told him she had been thinking of the stupid envelope. That's what they were calling it now, the stupid envelope. *What are you going to do with your money now that you can use it?*

He knew she had a few things on her mind, but she'd not made many decisions as yet. One of them was to purchase one of the buildings downtown and turned it into a shop. He knew that she'd be good at that as well.

Your dad said he'd gift me the smaller building that he owns. I think it would be perfect, but I don't want him to give it to me. He told her about how they'd given Trent the cabin in the woods when he'd gotten married. *That's what he said too. That it was a wedding gift. I pointed out that it wasn't for you but for me, and he said that you'd be happy if I was.*

I am and I would be. She snorted at him, and that's when he saw her. Moving slowly so that his wolf didn't make a sound, he stopped when she looked right at him. *You heard me.*

No, believe it or not, but I could smell you. He nodded, and she told him to close his eyes. *I'm going to try and hide this time. If you find me, I'll take something off. Not too much though. It's getting chilly.*

I'll warm you up. She was laughing in his head when he sat down and closed his eyes. *I'd take the building. If you don't, then Dad will hound you to death about it. I love him, but I tell you, once he gets something in his head, it's there until he gets what he wants.*

He told me that he wants grandchildren. He started to stand and go to her to find out what she said, but she continued. *I want children with you. But I'm not sure what sort of mom I'd be. And what happens to our child being that I'm part vamp and you're a full-blooded wolf?*

I don't care so long as they're happy and healthy. And I thought of something this morning. About how you can tell when someone isn't human. I think you can do that because of the vampire blood in your system. He stood up when he felt it had been long enough, and made his way to where he'd seen her last. *I can smell you stronger now. You're wet, aren't you?*

I am. And I've had to take off my panties because of it. His wolf snarled at him to get going after her. *Did you know that I don't have on a bra either? I thought that I'd be naked and fucked by now.*

Elijah leapt over the log in front of him, keeping his nose in the air to find her. Her scent was everywhere, it seemed. It was as if she'd sprayed each leaf with her juices just to confuse him. When he found what he thought was her footprint, he followed it until he saw her again.

She was indeed without her pants and panties. She also had taken off her shoes and socks. As he made his way to her, careful of where the wind was blowing, he jumped at her when she turned. His wolf held her down with his big body as he tore at her blouse.

He wants to eat you. She nodded and opened her legs for them. His wolf moved down her body to her pussy and sniffed at her. *Come for him, he needs it.*

As soon as she opened her legs wider for him, his wolf dove at her like he was going to tear into her skin. But instead of hurting her, he brought her three times with just his tongue at her clit. When he began taking her cream into his mouth by fucking her with his tongue, Noelle curled her fingers into his fur and held him to her.

His wolf seemed to be content with feasting on her. Elijah wanted her as well, and when his wolf let him go, he leaned over her, hard and aching. Fisting his cock, Elijah leaned back on his heels and watched her.

"Let me taste you." He wanted that as well and moaned when she wrapped her hand around him. "I've wanted to do this to you since the first time I saw you standing there naked for me."

"Anytime you want to suck on my cock, you go—Mother fuck."

She took him deep into her mouth, swallowing past the tight muscles in her throat until he could feel it wrapped around him. And every time she bobbed her head over him, he knew she was going to bring him quickly.

He held her to him when her fingers touched his balls, and when she cupped them in her hands, he jerked back. She looked up at him and asked him if she'd hurt him.

"No. Christ, no. I was ready to come, and that's not going to give you much if I do." She let go of his cock, and he heard a small pop sound. "I need to fuck you."

"You will when you come down my throat." She fisted him, and he saw stars. "Give me all of you, Elijah, and I will turn around and let you fuck me like an animal. Would you like that?"

It was all he could do just to get his head to nod at her. And when she took him in her mouth again, he noticed that she was no longer gentle but trying her best to bring him as quickly as she could. Even when her fingers slid along his balls, it wasn't until she gave them a small squeeze that he knew that he was done for.

He fucked her mouth harder then. Up on his knees now, he held her to him as he felt his balls tighten and his impending climax run along his spine. When she nipped at him, her teeth just grazing his sensitive skin, he came hard, his cock slamming down the back of her throat like he wanted to in her pussy.

Elijah saw stars and bursts of light in bright colors. He heard his wolf, begging him to take her so he could bite her again. He was sure that he was finished, that he'd come about all he could, when he looked down at her still holding his cock in her mouth.

Pulling her mouth from him was the hardest thing he'd ever done. He was hard still and getting harder, and he needed her. Turning her around so that her ass was in front of him, Elijah slammed forward into her pussy at the same time he slid his finger into her tight rosebud. Her screams had him wanting more.

"Come and I'll make it worth your while." She begged him for it now...whatever it was, she wanted it. "I'm going to bite you here, on your shoulder when you come. Then I'm going to empty my cock inside of you and fill you."

"Yes, please, now."

He told her that she had to come. Begged her to do so. As soon as she screamed again, he leaned over her and took her shoulders to the ground as he tore into her flesh.

Her taste was rich. The moment that he sucked her hot blood into his mouth, he knew what it was. She was ready. And more than likely they had created a child today. Fucking her harder now, needing to be sure that they had, Elijah saw lights again, bright and shiny when he came in her again.

Elijah didn't move when he was complete. That's what it felt like to him too, that he was complete. When he thought he could roll to his back to the ground without hurting her, he did so and held her to him even as his heart slowed. Now he had to figure out a way to tell her what they'd just done. Turning in his arms, she laid her head on his chest and yawned.

"Joe told me today." He didn't even bother asking her what Joe might have told her. "Your mom too. She was a lot more delicate about it than Joe, but she did finally get around to telling me that I was ready to have a child."

"I'm assuming that since you didn't stop me, that you're all right with that." She looked at him then. "I am, if you want to know."

"I am not sure, to be honest with you. I mean about having a child. But I do want them with you." He nodded, understanding completely. "Joe said that you'd be able to tell, but it might have been too late when you figured it out. I thought about mentioning it, but I was sort of afraid you'd tell me no."

"I want children, as many as we can have." She nodded, but there was more. He knew it. "The envelope, I was going to ask you what you think might be in it. Or did she tell you?"

"No, she didn't tell me. I'm not sure that she knows for sure, to be honest. I think that she believes there is money in it. But how much, I'm not sure." She nodded. "Are you afraid that it's something more?"

"No. I mean, it's not like he knew about me. And even if he did, I'm not sure that he would have wanted me either. I know what they said about him being bored and tired, but I can't think that I would have made any difference in his life."

Elijah lifted her chin up so that he could look at her. "What do you think a child of ours is going to do to us? Do you think that it'll make no difference in our lives? Are you thinking that it will mean little to us?"

"No, I'm going to love it with all that I am and then some. And I'll tell our child, every minute of every day, that I love it. But this isn't the same thing." He nodded. "No, he didn't know me."

"No, he might not have, but he did know your mom. And from what Noah told me, he was happy for a brief time after he met her. He knows this because he was with him right after he found her. Did you know that she was married at the time?" Noelle shook her head. "Yes, the man she was married to wasn't a great guy, not abusive, but not very ambitious. And when you were conceived, it was his idea to have you given up or aborted. He had no idea that you weren't his, Noah said. But once he died, your mother kept you, loving you despite the fact that she was poor and alone."

"Then she met Howard." He nodded. "He wasn't good to her either, was he? He had an affair after my mom married him, and then she died."

"Joe is going to find out what happened there. She said that she only has to touch Howard to find out what your mom was like. She has it in her head that someplace in the house you lived is something of hers for you. Pictures or something." Noelle sat up then, excited. "If it's there, then she can find it."

"A picture would be wonderful. I don't remember a thing about her." He nodded, and when she stood up and began to dress in her blouse, he watched her until she turned to him. "You need to come with me. I have to think what I'm going to do with our money."

"All right, but if you mean the lottery winnings, that's all yours to do with as you see fit. I want you to have fun with it."

He was laughing as they made their way back through the woods. Every time she would find an article of her clothing, he watched her struggle to put it on. Once she found her pants, she had to take off both her boots to pull them on. Elijah had never been so entertained by someone dressing before. By the time they got to the house, he was as excited as she was.

~~~

"She's here. Noah told us that Helenia had arrived earlier this morning." Noelle wasn't sure what she was to do now, but she knew that she would do anything to help. When Sterl sat down in the chair by her desk, she wanted to get up and hug him. "I just came from talking to the rest of them and was walking home when I saw you were here. How is it going? Dad said he gave you a desk."

"They found it in one of the buildings that they were working in. I guess it's really old." He nodded. It occurred to her that he was very outwardly calm, but she also knew that he was dealing in his own way. "Elijah said that you were invited to go back to teaching. But that you were going to start in a lower grade this time."

He got up then, moving around the room, touching some of the things that she'd brought over, other items that had been brought to her by TJ or one of the others. He picked up the box of chalk that she'd purchased on her way in this morning.

"Fifth grade math. I have to figure out how to win against her by hurting her first. I'm not sure I know how to do that." She nodded, trying to keep up. "What if I can't do it?"

"Do what, Sterl?" He said teach. "I think you're going to do very well at it. Most of your students already know you, don't they? I mean, you've grown up in this town."

"I did. All of us did." He started drawing on the large chalkboard that had also been unearthed in one of the other buildings. "They don't use these in the classrooms any more. It's smartboards. All computer run and much easier. I don't want to die, Noelle."

"I don't want you to either, Sterl. I've grown to love you a great deal in the last weeks." He nodded, still not moving from where he was standing. As he worked on the board, she watched him. "You can win this against her. You know that, don't you?"

"No." The single word broke her heart. Getting up, she looked at what he had been doing and knew that it was an animal, but was not sure which. "I'd very much like to come and work with you here. To see these old things brought back to life. If I get through this with Helenia, I'm going to think about going back to teaching. I'm not sure yet."

The drawing was magnificent. Even with the single color that he had, he'd managed to bring the beauty of the wolf to life. She stood in front of it, wondering if he'd had colors what the picture would have held.

"I used to draw all the time when I was a kid. It relaxed me in a lot of ways." When he picked up the eraser to no doubt run it over the drawing, she stopped him. "Someone will see it."

"I should hope a lot of people see it." When she put out her hand, he handed her the eraser. "Elijah is working with Doug today on the specs for the building. I was going to go to a few estate sales, as well as a couple of auctions. Were you serious about wanting to work with me? I could use a big strong man to help me lift and tote today."

"I'd really like that." When he grinned at her, she could see the Sterl that she was sure had been missing for a long time. "But you have to buy me lunch. Since I've been...since this thing finished up with me, I've picked up my appetite."

"Deal." She reached to Elijah. *Sterl is with me and we're going to go on a hunt. I don't know when we'll be home, but I have an idea that we'll be kind of late. He wants to work with me. And did you know that he drew?*

His laughter made her realize how disjointed she'd sounded. *I'm glad that my brother is with you, and if you're too late, call me please. And yes, he mentioned that he wanted to work with you in the shop. I'm assuming that he doesn't mean the job you have with Trent.* She told him she thought that one was finished. *I doubt it. Not with Trent. And yes, I knew that he drew. He's really good at it. I wondered for a long time why he didn't go into that rather than teaching.*

I'm going to work on him. She gathered her coat and purse. *He drew me a wolf on the chalk board. I think I'm going to have him paint some things in our windows here. It would attract a lot of customers.*

I'm sure by the end of the day, not only will you have him drawing again, but giving art lessons to the elderly. She loved that idea and told him. *I was joking, love. But you and Sterl have fun. I'm sure that you both could use it, and be careful. You remember what Noah said, she's weak and stupid but can hurt you.*

Yes, I remember.

As they got into Sterl's truck she asked him about it. She'd never had much of a car and even when she had one, it was a piece of shit.

"I was actually thinking of selling this one. It's old, so it's really not worth much, but it runs well. What if I showed you how to drive it and then you can use it for the shop? That way I get a tax break and you get something to use." She laughed and told him she would do it. "Good. Perhaps you should think of getting something for yourself too. With the baby coming and all."

"You know?" He nodded and told her it was her scent. "Oh. I guess I give off all kinds of clues that I have no idea about. Can I ask you why it is that no one hugs me? I mean, for such a loving family, no one hugs the women. Why is that?"

"We're possessive. I mean, we will kill someone if they touch what we consider ours. And when you're hugged, the other person's scent is all over you. It can make our wolves very pissy." She thought about that. "And with you breeding, it's doubly hard on the wolf with someone else's scent on you."

It was a lot to think about, this wolf thing, but she let it go, knowing that sometime after the baby was born she'd be converted and understand more. As they pulled up in front of the first house where the tag sale was going on, she looked at him.

"Have you ever dickered with anyone before?" He said he hadn't. When it was priced, he paid it. "Well, don't do that today. Nothing is ever marked what they really want for it. And if you pay full price for something, then we're not going to make much. Remember, we have to sell this, and if we break even, we won't be in business for very long. And I have a list of things that your dad asked me to find as well. Can you look for them for me?"

She handed him the list, and he nodded. Some of the things on TJ's list were things she had no knowledge of. Noelle had taken the list and looked some of them up, thinking that he'd been having fun with her. But there really was a bastard file, as well as a macaroni tool. She was glad that Sterl was willing to find them.

By the time they were both ready for lunch, not only had they found most of the things on TJ's list, but a lot of items for the shop. She'd found most of hers in the second place they'd stopped, and Sterl had even managed to find himself a couple of items as well for his own home. As they were entering the diner, he told her that he was going to take her up on her idea about the art classes.

"I know how to paint as well. I have a few canvases at the house that I've played around with for a while. A lot of them, well a few anyway, I'll never show, but I have a few fluff pieces as well." She'd noticed that he'd bought a box of paints as well as a few dozen paint brushes. It had made him so happy that he'd gotten them for less than the sticker said that she didn't have the heart to tell him she might have gotten a better deal. "I noticed that you're not using all of the building, the second floor. Do you think you can rent it out to me? I'd really like to paint up there."

"I'd be glad to have you up there. It would give me someone to talk to when no one is around." He told her she was going to do well. "I'm not so sure. I mean, I love buying things that I can put in there, but who is going to want a stack of tea towels with flowers embroidered on them? I just thought they were pretty."

"They were. And I bet it's one of the first things you sell." She didn't think she'd sell much of anything, but smiled at him. He was looking younger all the time. After ordering a huge lunch, she asked him about his house. "Mom and Dad helped me buy it. Which is good because after I was hurt, there was no way for me to live at home with all the stairs. I haven't done much to it. I have no idea why, because it's old and needs a lot of work, but I'll get to it. I think that I'll be able to fill it with some of the things we saw today. I like the older, primitive things we saw."

"Elijah wants to do some things to our house." She grinned. "I have a hard time thinking of it as our house. Anyway, he wants to enlarge the dining area, as well as put in a new fireplace in the living room. I love the house the way it is, but I can understand why it's not going to be big enough. He's had to hold off Myra from just doing it for him."

"She scares the shit out of me." Noelle laughed as her sandwich and fries were set in front of her. Sterl had two large meatball subs and a double order of fries. She'd learned that too, that they could eat all they wanted and not gain an ounce. "But I like her. Despite her clothing choices, I really do like her."

When they were finished eating, he paid the check. His reasoning was that he'd had such a wonderful time that he wanted to give her something. They were still laughing as they made their way to the truck and on to the next few houses.

CHAPTER 11

Scott wasn't sure what was wrong with the couple in front of him, but he was positive that he'd missed something. Every time he had to tell the man, the Dom for them, that he was to order his sub to do what he wanted, not just hit her, he would get more upset with him. Finally, when he'd had enough, Scott stood in front of him.

"What do you think you're doing? Get out of my way. This is what she likes."

Scott had no idea why, but he had a feeling the man was using sexual play for a license to beat the woman with him.

"I don't think she's enjoying this as much as you think she is." He turned to look at the woman curled into a tight ball. "You're not supposed to simply hurt her, but to bring her pleasure with this. All you're doing is causing her a great deal of pain."

"She likes pain." Scott thought it was more like she was used to it rather than any kind of enjoyment. "Get on back over there and watch us. That way when I take her, you know that she's doing it right."

He'd said that before, wanting Scott to watch him while he fucked the woman. There wasn't supposed to be any kind of sexual contact in here. And even if there was, Scott wasn't going to watch this man. Yes, there were times when one or both of the partners would have a climax, a powerful one too. But there wasn't any intercourse. His business wasn't a brothel, but a place to come for guidance on how to give both partners pleasure. The man picked up the whip Scott had taken from him twice already, and Scott decided that enough was enough.

"The session is over. I think that it's time that you left."

The man stared at him, and Scott knew that he was going to be trouble. Touching his hand to the button that would bring him help, he was knocked back when the man hit him in the face with a chair. Scott hit the floor and was up again before the man could do more harm to him.

As the doors exploded open, Scott moved out of the way of the man as he came at him again. He never knew their names, only that he called them Dom or Sub. Today he wished he'd had something more than that, as this was about to get ugly.

The Dom took out three of Scott's employees, knocking them against the wall and heavy equipment before he grabbed the sub by the hair and started to drag her to the bars. Blood was making it hard for him to see, but he hit the man twice before he finally let her go. This time when he turned on Scott, he was ready for him. Two punches—one from him, the other from Elijah, who just seemed to appear in the room—and the Dom finally went down. Scott fell to the floor, feeling every one of the hits now that it was over.

The police arrived ten minutes later. He knew both of them, but it was no less stressful for him. This was the third time in less than a month that someone had called in the police for a customer who had the wrong idea as to what he was there for. When Elijah handed him an ice pack, he looked around.

"I'm too fucking old for this shit." Elijah just laughed. "I'm sick of people too. I think I'm going to take the land that Mom and Dad gave me next to where Trent has the cabin and live there for the rest of my life."

"Nah, you'd miss me. But I'm just glad I was close enough to come and help you. He was out to kill you, I think." Scott wasn't even sure what his problem had been. "The woman that he was with, she's pressing charges too. Not against you, but the man. Apparently, he's had her in his basement for a couple of weeks doing all sorts of things to her. The police are headed there now."

"Christ." As he was helped up, he walked around the damage and thought he really was going to close his doors after this. "Two of my guys are going to the hospital. Lucy, who runs the desk, said she's done, and I'm pretty sure that my insurance company is going to laugh at me when I asked them again to replace some of this shit. I'm done too."

"Good." He had expected something more from his brother, but was glad that he'd not had to justify himself to him. Elijah had always been the most supportive of his brothers. "Do you want to come and work for me?"

"Doing what? I have no idea how to tell if a business is going to make it. And I'm way too jaded right now to hear a sob story about why someone's business is failing." Elijah told him of the plans he had concerning his house. "Seriously? I can do that. I loved working with the builders when I had some things done to my house. Trent did a great job, but I wanted something else in the bedrooms."

"I'm sure I don't want to know." Scott said nothing. They knew that he liked it rough. You didn't live in a small town without everyone knowing your business. But his bedroom was normal. There was a bed, two dressers, as well as a couple of chairs. The only thing he'd wanted different was the closet. It had been made for someone who wore a lot of nicer clothing than he owned. "Anyway, I'd like to start as soon as we can manage it. I have a lot of work on my plate right now with Trent being gone on that retreat with some of the pack members. But if you can give me a few hours a week, I would love it."

"All right. I'd love that too." As he was leading the police around the room where everything had happened, he also offered them the tapes of the day. After they left, he was sitting in his own office when Elijah came in the room with him. "I'm really going to do it. I just got off the phone with my lawyer, and she's going to put this place on the market for me."

"Will you miss it?" Scott shook his head. "I love going to work every day. I mean really love it, but lately, with having Noelle at the house with me, it's getting harder and harder. I don't want to sell out, but I think I'm going to find some people to work for me that can take some of the load off. I want to be with her all the time, and I find that to be more fun as well."

"I thought of that too. Getting more people to come in and do what I do. Be the boss and not be working. But I really have had enough. It's hard to maintain a life when you're trying to help people with theirs. I just need to cut ties and move on." Scott leaned back in his chair, feeling pretty good after saying it aloud. "I think this has been a long time in coming. For both of us."

"Yes, I think you're right." Elijah told him what Noelle was doing today with Sterl. "She'll bring him out of his shell. Not that I don't think he will come out anyway, but this will help him. Joe is wonderful, but she knows too much about him. Noelle is sort of the girl next door type, and he might say things to her that he'd not to us."

"He's going to open a studio over her shop. I think he'll do well at that. I'm not sure that teaching kids is something that he's going to go back to. He's seen too much." Scott nodded. "Randal, however, was born to be a teacher. Christ, how many years has it been that he's been teacher of the year? Ten?"

"About that. Yes, I agree, Randal is suited to being a teacher more than most I know. And he cares. Mom told me that he's set up a food pantry in his room for kids that might not have lunch. They have to pay for it by bettering themselves in some way. Two days ago a child wanted one of those pudding things and to pay for it. He had to make a good grade on his test. I guess he did so well on it that Randal had a party for the entire class. And the single moms just think he's the best thing since sliced bread."

"Mom told me that his last parent teacher conference ended early because a bunch of the women, both married and single, had cornered him. I almost feel sorry for him." Scott did as well. And was envious too. "Do you date much, big brother?"

"Not really. I mean I go out, but only when I have no choice in the matter. Pack functions mostly. Occasionally Mom will set me up with a date for something. But I don't socialize all that much anymore. I'm must be really getting old." Elijah asked him about a mate. "Do you really think that we all have one out there? I mean, someone for all of us, and she's just waiting to come here and change our lives?"

"I do. I might not have a month ago, but I do believe that now." Scott wasn't so sure. "Will you welcome her should she find you?"

"Welcome? I'd probably fall down at her feet just for the chance to get laid on a regular basis." He realized how crude that sounded. "I'm sorry. I'm just a little stressed out. I think I'm going to go home, shift, and run until I fall asleep in the woods. I've not been doing that as much as I should either. My wolf hates me."

"I doubt that he hates you, but I'm betting he wants to get laid once in a while as well."

Scott thought he might be right. As they gathered up the few things that he didn't want to leave in an empty building, Elijah said he'd come back and help him load up the rest tomorrow. Scott was feeling better and better about this.

As the two of them made their way to his truck, Scott looked around, feeling tense all of a sudden. Something was off. He wasn't sure what it was, but he felt it. Looking at Elijah, he was sure that he did as well. The air even tasted a little off.

Do you see anything? Elijah told him that he didn't, but to act normal. *And what is that exactly, this normal you speak of?*

When the man came out of the shadows, neither of them moved. Scott could feel his wolf ready for whatever came their way, but Elijah put his hand on his arm when he moved toward the man. As he curled back in the shadows, a term that Scott thought was perfect, he had to fight with his wolf to not go and hunt him down.

I don't think he wants anyone to see us talking to him. Or maybe just one person not to know. Scott asked Elijah how he knew that. *I have no idea. But I think he wants us to go to him, but make it look like we're doing this on our own.*

And you got all that because of some guy poking his head out of the darkness? And so you know, if you think you're going in that dark building by yourself, then you're fucking nuts. Elijah told him he wasn't. *Good.*

You're going with me. When he started to protest that wasn't what he meant, Elijah moved toward where the man had been. Vampire, his mind screamed at him, and he hesitated just a little.

You're going to be safe. Nothing will hurt you. Noah laughed when Scott started cursing. *Does your mom know you talk like that?*

Yes. I don't do it in front of her, but I'm pretty sure she knows. Where the fuck are you, and how do you know that it's safe to follow this man? He told him he was there as well. *Why didn't you come out instead of letting a stranger do this?*

Because he's not yet aware that I'm here. He has information for Sterling, and he's passing it on. I'm here to make sure that he gets to tell you before Helenia figures it out. I'm watching him.

Scott moved into the building behind his brother. The vampire wasn't anyone that they knew, but he stayed back in the corner like he was afraid of them. Noah assured them that he was.

"I know where that monster is. She's hiding out in the cemetery where she don't belong." Elijah asked him who he was talking about. "That white thing. The one that is making one of the tombs that we been using her own. Killed two of my friends by throwing them out in the sun before I managed to get on her better side. I don't trust her, but she needed me and I came to do her bidding."

"And how did you know to come talk to one of us?" Scott nearly told Elijah, but was told to wait by Noah. "You just happened to stick your head out when we were in the lot and just happened to have information about this woman that you think we might need? I don't believe you."

"She cut me." Scott felt fear roll over him and his wolf. "If I show you, will you hurt me? It can't heal until she gets what she wants. And that is to tell you where she's at."

"Show us." Scott turned on his phone using the flashlight app to see the man. When he cringed away from it, Scott moved it to his body and not his face. The man lifted his shirt up, and Scott staggered back a little.

"She said that once I gave you the message that I knew where she was, then she'd help me." Scott asked him if he thought she'd do that. "No. I don't. But I have a way of taking care of it myself. I've seen what she's done to others that disobey her."

"You weren't to show us what she did, were you?" The man shook his head. "Is she really there? At the cemetery?"

"She is, but not in the tomb of Flowers. You'll have to figure out the rest. If I say it, she'll know what I'm about." He looked behind him, and Scott wondered if there were more like him here. "The walls here, they sure could use a nice coat of paint, don't you think? But I'd have a look at them with the light thing you have and not the sun. The sun can take things away."

Just as Scott was going to ask him what he meant, he moved by them. The speed at which he did so made Scott think that he'd gone into the sunlight quickly so that he'd not be able to change his mind. The screams from the man were cut off abruptly, and Scott looked at his brother.

"He killed himself rather than go back and tell her that he'd done it." Elijah said he had. Pulling out his phone, he asked him what he'd meant by the walls. "I think there might be a message. I have no idea why I think that, but I'm completely weirded out, and that's the first thing that popped into my head."

Using his own phone, he looked at the walls behind where the man had been. When he found it, he realized why the man had said to do it with their phones and not the sunlight they could have used. The vampire had used his own blood to help them.

"Did you know about this?" Noah said that he hadn't when he joined them. "Do you think this is the tomb that she's using, or a trap?"

"I think the man gave his life to rid the area of her, and this would be his way of helping." Scott nodded at Noah. "I've never been to the cemetery, but do you suppose there are many of the tombs with the name Jefferson on them?"

Scott didn't know either, but they were one step closer to taking this bitch out. "We'll do this the easy way first. Find someone that works there and get a list of the tombs and names. That way we have a general idea of where we're headed."

"I have an idea." Scott looked at his brother and decided that while he'd help him, he didn't think this was an idea that was going to bode well for someone. He was glad it wasn't going to be him too. "I have to talk to Trent and Sterl, but this might be a way to end this shit without us walking into a trap that might get one of us hurt. Yeah, this will be good."

Making their way out of the building, he opened the door wide and watched as the words there burned off and turned to ash. Scott wondered at the fear one would have to rather die than to face her. He hoped that this thing went as well as Myra and the others were telling them it would.

~~~

Helenia was feeling stronger every day. She'd forgotten that she could do nicely with some anger to power her. And here in this nest there was a great deal of it. Its power would feed her slowly, but at the rate these vampires were going, she would be up and going in no time. This might be the reason, she thought, that Noah had never lived in a den of vampires. They were worse than some children she'd seen playing. Christ, she hated children almost as much as she did Noah.

The man that she'd sent to find the alpha was going to be dead as soon as he got back here. He was going to be anyway, but she'd planned to just slice him up and watch him turn to dust. Now he was going to suffer for making her wait for so fucking long. And Helenia had been at this long enough. She knew just how to make a vampire last a good long time before he was no more.

"Mistress." She looked at the young vampire when he spoke behind her. "I have a connection with Darrell."

"What the hell is a Darrell, and why do you think I'd care?" He told her that he was the one he'd sent out yesterday. "And why is he contacting you and not me? I do hope he knows that I'm not going to be happy with him when he returns."

"He's not. Returning, I mean. He's met with the sun." As the vampire walked away from her, she was sure she heard him laugh. Letting her temper go, she lashed out at him and the group that seemed to share a very small brain, and killed them all.

Her rage was shifting to something stronger and quicker to ignite, she'd only just realized today. Just this morning she'd gone into the town to find her alpha, and she'd noticed that every shop was closed up and there was not a single person in the area. Small towns did that, she knew, rolled up their sidewalks seemingly at a certain hour in the evening, but it was daylight on a Saturday morning. Smiling, she thought of the damage she'd done anyway.

The two buildings that were closest to her had been set on fire. She had no idea what might have been in them, nor did she care, but the heat coming off her had felt wonderful, the power of it exhilarating. Helenia decided that she loved this new her. And her temper was going to give her a lot of pleasure.

Moving out of the tomb she'd taken for herself, she thought of Noah and him commanding her to come to him. She'd been here for two days now and nothing. Helenia wondered if he'd even called to her, and her mind had only made that up when she'd been hurt. Stranger things were going on with her, and she wasn't going to believe that anyone as weak as Noah would have enough power to pull her here.

The alpha was here too. This was the little town where she'd first noticed him. Smiling, she thought of the things she was going to do with him. First and foremost, she was going to fuck him. After she had enough of that, she was going to cage him and find a lab that she could work with. He'd be weak, of that there was no doubt. Helenia had poisoned not just his mind but his blood as well. But he'd be hers to use and to create all the monsters that she wanted.

Her idea had been born when she'd been watching a battle between men. It had been huge; many lives had been taken. But her thoughts had been, why bother with just killing each other off? Why not make it fun as well? Then a wolf had come onto the scene, his huge body dark with the blood of the fallen, and she'd watched him, excited beyond anything she'd been in a long while as he ate the dying. He'd not bothered with the dead, which made her realize he loved his meat fresh, but had torn at the victims while they fought with him to keep their body. Then when some other animals came for his tasty treat, he'd killed them as well, tearing out their throats and letting them bleed out. Helenia knew then that she had to find her a shifter alpha wolf to do her bidding.

"He'll be mine, and when I have used him up, I'll toss him at Noah's feet, his body nothing but a shell." Smiling, she made her way to the building where she had smelled the wolf.

Today there was something different about it. She walked around it three times before it occurred to her what it was. There was a For Sale sign in front of it. The name of the realtor was there, with a number, and Helenia wondered what had happened. Had her alpha closed it down, this place of slavery? She would have to open it again, order him to do so. Then something else occurred to her.

He would command a legion. He was a pack leader, a wolf who would have others to do his bidding. With her commanding them all, she would not have any use for labs and men in coats.

Following the scent that was a wolf, she found the building where the vampire had met the sun. Stupid bastard had thwarted her fun. But as she looked around, she saw evidence that someone had painted arrows on the floor. Stepping around the markings, not touching whatever magic had put it there, she found herself standing in front of a large map. And it had a picture of a house as well as the drawing of a wolf. There were other pictures too, and it took her a few moments to figure out someone had left her a message.

She thought the drawing of her was quite good. The monster that they'd made of her had her thinking that they understood that she was superior to them by far. Then the feet drawn along a line indicated, she supposed, that she was to go to the house. And the picture of the wolf had to mean that he lived in this house. Smiling, she thought that if her vampire were alive, she might have killed him quickly for doing this for her. Helenia had made a good impression on him, and that satisfied her to no end.

"Do I go or not?" That was a good question, she thought to herself. Was it a trap? Not that it mattered. She was by far stronger than any of them. Even if Noah were there, he was too afraid of her and her power to come out and stand against her. And if he were, it would be his last stand. Deciding to go, she studied the map more and thought she had it. Then she took the drawing of herself.

"Just too good not to take." Smiling, she left the building and went to the one next door. It smelled of sex and wolf. Snapping her fingers, she set a flame to it and frowned when all it did was fizzle out. After trying four more times with no results, Helenia moved on. "Waste of power anyway. I might need the little it would take to destroy it."

Helenia would no longer need the lab, not that she'd figured out how to make that work anyway. But when she took her alpha, and she would, then he would control all wolves, men, and beasts simply because of the power he would have in her. This was much better, much, much better than she'd ever thought of before.

CHAPTER 12

Sterl thought the plan was a good one...brilliant, as a matter of fact, but he was no less terrified that it wasn't going to work. He'd seen this monster. These people had not. Moving to stand by the window of his studio, he wondered if he'd been too rash in setting this up.

"I'm not going to allow you to be negative about this." Sterl turned and looked at the woman standing there. He'd not seen her in a whole year, yet there she stood looking just as beautiful. "You don't have a hug for your old grandma?"

"First of all, you will never be old, and secondly, you told me some time ago that I was much too strong to give you the kind of hugs I love." She waved him off and told him to get over here. "Grandma, when did you get in? I'm assuming Mom called you?"

"Your grandda had a hankering to come and aggravate his only son, and I thought we'd come now so that when you beat this bitch, we can be here to celebrate. Trent told us what was going on." Sterl nodded but hadn't moved to hug her. "What is it, my boy? You think you can't win this? I do."

"I don't think they're taking this as seriously as they should. Elijah has it all worked out, but I'm not sure that she'll follow along like they think she will." She moved to him, and Sterl did the same toward her. "I have missed you so much, Grandma."

"And I you. Oh my, you have grown up." They hugged; he was gentle with her in that she was a full two feet shorter than him, and tiny in stature. When he held her, just looking down at her, she wiped at his cheek. "Don't worry. I promise you that there is not a person here, wolf or otherwise, that isn't taking this seriously. And your grandda is over at the house now, going over every detail about it. You know him and plans."

"Yes. I know. I think that's where Elijah got it from." She nodded and they sat down on his couch. The studio also had a small cot in it, something that he'd found when he'd been moving things around, and had decided that he liked it. "How long are you here for this time? I'm assuming that you are still touring the world."

"I think I've seen enough for the time being. I have seen things and.... Well, things that I can't believe. Humans can be strange, don't you think?" He nodded. "I do love that Joe. My goodness, she is powerful. And Noelle. And to think I'm going to be a great grandma in a few months. And TJ is as smitten with them both as he was with Christina when she came along."

"Noelle and I have been hanging out together while Elijah works. She owns the shop downstairs that deals in odds and ends. It's called Second Time Around. Dad had been finding things around the buildings that we all own in the area and bringing them to her. I think he's buying things up and telling her that he found them." Grandma said that sounded like something he'd do. "Mom is knitting booties. She's not all that good at it, I don't think, but she's having fun learning. Joe has been working with her on it."

"I tried to teach her once, but she was too busy with you boys to give it much of a go. I have been knitting too. I have boxes of things for each of you boys." She looked at him with that glint in her eyes that he recognized, and laughed. "I know you have no mate as yet, but she'll come along."

"I just want this over with." She asked him about the canvases that he'd set up. "I've been painting. Not much and it's not very cheery, but I actually feel better after I'm done."

He got up to show her the one he was working on. When she stood too and came to look at it closer, he looked at it as well. It was part of the dreams he'd had when he'd been possessed by the monster.

The scene looked pretty enough, he supposed, if you only glanced at it. But if someone looked deeper, really studied the painting, they could see more. There was the tree he was hanging from, the car deep in the dense forest. Even the blood staining the grasses where his friends had been murdered. They weren't in the picture yet. He wasn't even sure that they would be added, but he was there, as was the monster.

"You.... Oh Sterling, this is powerful." He watched her face as she reached out to nearly touch the paint there. He knew that she was aware that it was still wet, but he could tell that she wanted to. "I want to take you out of here, grab you out of the tree, and pull you into my arms and keep you safe."

Sterl knew that of all the people in the world, his grandma would get him the best. She'd always been there for all of them, but Sterl knew that if he had a problem or a question about something, anything really, that he could go to her and she'd give him the answer. No matter how embarrassing or painful it would be to either of them.

"I have two more." He had never shown these to anyone before. It had been in his mind to just paint them, then put them away. It was therapy for him, the feeling that if he put it to canvas, then it would somehow lessen the pain that was still there. It had in a way, but he still hurt. "They're finished, I suppose you could call them, but I'm not sure yet what I'm going to do with them."

"You'll put them in a gallery. And I noticed that you signed it simply with your first initial. I like that. Leaves you to keep a low profile when you make it big." That was another thing that he loved most about his grandma — both of his grandparents, actually — that they could encourage him in ways that would make him feel that he could do whatever it was. His parents did as well, very much so, but Grandma made it sound like a done deal. He set the other two up against the wall under the window.

When she didn't say anything, he felt the need to fill in the silence. "I know this one is very black, dark I guess. It's the day after the accident. I kind of blurred the faces — I don't want anyone to know that it was myself and Trent there — but I think it still shows the anguish. They tied me down too. I think...it's what I felt like with her in my head. Tied down."

This time she did touch the painting, his face and then his wrists. When she turned to him, his heart broke for making her cry, and when she held him, he cried as well. Then without a word, she pulled back and looked at the third painting.

He knew every stroke of it, even the way that he'd worked hard to get the red right. The blood there needed to be perfect. It was of the day that Myra had come and taken away all of the poison from his mind.

"You bled that day as well." Sterl nodded. "So much of it too. I know that it was necessary, but I want to hunt her down and hurt her for harming my baby boy."

His face in the painting was once again blurred, but he wasn't sure that anyone could see anything but the blood on his face anyway. Even his ears had leaked out some of his blood, but it was his hands that drew his attention. In them he'd put a gun and a knife. The gun at his head, the knife at his throat. It was his way of showing that he was finished with life. Done with all the pain.

"I felt relieved when I was finished with this one. I know that she's out there still, that I might not survive this, but this is what I feel all the time. Even now, with all the poison taken from me, I still am so tired of this." He looked out the window and down at the people on the streets. "It's not a constant thing now. This feeling of wanting to die, it lessens all the time. But it's there, just on the outer circle of my life."

"You need to see someone. A doctor. He can help you like no one can." He knew she was right, but he'd never do that. Who would he see that he could be honest with? No one. They just wouldn't understand him. "Sterling, look at me."

He did but he felt pained by her sadness. "Grandma, she's coming here. Probably today or tomorrow, but she's going to go to the house and confront us."

"Good." He nodded and looked out the window. "What do you think she's going to see when she arrives, Sterling? I can answer that for you. She's going to see a strong being, stronger than when she hurt him. A family that will be there for him, and has been there right there with him through it all. This thing, this monster that you drew here? She's going to know a reckoning that she's never felt before. And when it's done, you're going to be stronger for it."

"I don't know." She turned him around and smacked him across the cheek. He knew that he deserved it, but asked why anyway.

"You won't talk like that. You're my Sterling Calhoun, and you will be strong. If you let her win, then she will. If you know that you can beat her? Then you fucking will." He cocked a brow at her cursing. "Yes, I used the word. And I will again if you make me. Now, I want you to get busy with your life, and then when she gets here, deal with her as quickly and as efficiently as I know you do everything in your life. Do you understand me?"

"Yes, ma'am." When he opened his mouth to tell her that she'd hurt him once, Grandma lifted her hand. Sterling had to smile. "When did you become all tough and sassy?"

"I've been living with your grandda all on my own for the last eight months. That's enough to make anyone grow some." He laughed when she did. "Now that's what I wanted to see. And so you know, I'm going to see about finding you a gallery for these and whatever else you paint. Sterling, you are going to be famous."

"I just want to be free." She nodded, and this time when she put her hand to his cheek, he felt her love. "I love you so very much, Grandma."

"And I do you as well, Sterling. But if you make me have to get upset with you again over this, I'm going to tan your hide for you." He nodded and hugged her to him. "You're going to be just fine, Sterling. Just as fine as rain."

He hoped so. Sterl really did hope so. As they made plans to go to his mom's house, Sterl thought of the empty canvases that he'd bought this morning, and the paints that had shown up on his table. He was sure that Noelle had done it, and he loved her all the more for helping him.

~~~

Elijah could hear Noelle in the shower. She was crying again. He wasn't sure what she was upset about, but knew that she'd been dealing with it her way, hiding out for a few days now. He'd talked to his mom about it, and she told him to just be there for her. Whatever it was, she'd share it when she was ready and not before. Getting up, he decided that he liked his dad's idea better. Confront her.

Pulling open the shower door, he watched her as she tried to hide from him. He let her for a few minutes, then stepped under the spray to hold her. When she curled around him, both with her arms and legs, he knew that this was the right way to fix it.

"Tell me, love. Tell me what it is. I can't stand to see you hurting like this." She cried all the harder and held him tightly. "I love you, Noelle. I swear that whatever it is, we can overcome it."

"He hurt them." Elijah didn't know who had hurt who, but he had a feeling it was her father. "When they were younger and would tell him what I'd done or said to them that day, the nice things, he would hurt them for it. Daniel called me Monday and said he wanted to talk, and we did."

He'd known that. Casen had told him that she'd gotten a call from someone and had gone out right after. When she'd returned some four hours later, he had said that something terrible had happened. But when Elijah had asked, she told him she was just nervous about the baby. But the crying had started the next morning.

"Daniel has left the area. Did you know that? That he'd left the day Howard was arrested? Ron is gone too. They're together for now." He knew that Daniel had left, but not that the younger one had as well. "He's trying to make it on his own. I guess he's got a job now, as well as a place of his own. His first."

"Did he ask you for help?" Elijah thought of how hard it would have been for him to start over and felt sorry for him. "We can help him out if that's what he wants."

"He only wanted my forgiveness." Elijah took the shampoo from her and poured some in his palm to wash her hair while she continued. "Daniel said that he and Ron are living together right now and it's been hard to find work. But he's been working at a fast food place for a few days now and Ron is still looking. The problem that he is having is that he has a record, and he doesn't have any work experience for anyone to check on."

Elijah washed her hair, running his fingers through the soft strands as he tried to think of something to say. He wasn't sure that he could ever forgive either man for their part in his mate's pain, but if she wanted to help them, he would do whatever she wanted.

"What did you tell him when he asked for you to forgive him?" When she didn't answer him, he picked up the big sponge that had only just recently made it into their bathroom and poured some soft soap over it. Running it down her spine and over her ass, he felt his cock stretch and told it to behave. "Honey, is that what has you upset?"

"He won't take anything from me. He said that he's taken enough from people and he wants to do this on his own." Elijah nodded, thinking that was the smartest thing the man could say, and he respected him for it. "I didn't tell him about the money or anything, but I told him I was working and that I had my own money, but he said no. And Ron said that if they couldn't make it by themselves, then they didn't deserve to. I think that's what hurts me so much. That Howard never taught them anything about being a good person, and they're getting it despite him."

"I have an idea how we can help both of them and not hurt their pride. Trent and the rest of us need to hire a crew to work out at the new site to clear the land. We're doing it, with Doug's okay, to get the wood. A lot of the homes on the pack land heat with it, and then there is the added idea that we could sell the lumber to someone and put the money back into the ones that help." She turned and looked at him then. "It pays well. There is also insurance, as well as housing that could be theirs if they come to help out. When the land is cleared, they'll have a job reference that looks better than anything they can get working where they are, as well as they can save up for a place to buy. I'd even help them with that if this works out."

"Why?" He asked her what she meant. "Why are you going to do this for them? I didn't ask you to."

"No. You didn't. But if they're willing to help themselves, then I'd like to help them as well. Mostly it's only to give them the opportunity to do something for themselves. If they fuck up or just quit, there are any number of people to take their place. I'll get them in. It's entirely up to them what they do afterwards."

"I love you." He grinned at her and leaned down to kiss her. "You're going to get pretty lucky if you keep that up."

"Promise?" Elijah kissed her again, this time picking her up to wrap around him. "We could both get pretty lucky if you play your cards right. Turn around and let me wash you. I find that to be very sexy, watching the soap run down over the curves of your body." He put her down and told her to stand very still while he took care of her.

The soapy sponge was his new best friend. As he moved it over her neck to her breasts, he felt his mouth water to follow the path that the pretty pink bubbles traveled, the way the sponge seemed to curve around each of her muscles and soft skin. When he had one breast as clean as he could manage it, he took the tip in his mouth as he moved the sponge down over her navel to her hips and between her thighs.

Her fingers curled in his hair, her hand around his cock. Rocking into her palm, he moved the sponge over her, feeling her riding it. As he lifted his head, she continued to fist him, her hand sliding over his tip only to go to his root in a smooth continuous motion.

"I love the way you feel. Soft and silky, hard and thick." He moaned when she dropped to her knees in front of him. "I need to have you. Sit down."

He wasn't sure if he sat or fell back to the shower seat when she took him into her mouth. And she didn't slow either, not when he put his hand to her head to pull her back, nor when he begged her to let him finish inside of her. Noelle made him so close to paradise one second, then sobbing with the need to come the next. And when he came, shouting out her name as she held his balls in her hand, he was sure that he'd never had this much pleasure, had never loved anyone as he did her, and that for as long as he lived, Noelle would be his only one true love.

"Come here. I can't stand up yet." Her giggle seemed to give him more strength. Standing up, jerking her body to his, Elijah lifted her up and slammed his cock deep into her when he pressed her against the wall. "Christ, come for me. I'm not going to last."

She came three times, quick, hard, tight punches that left him as drained as she seemed to be. But he needed her, to mark her. And when she bit down on his shoulder, screaming around the flesh, Elijah tilted her head and bit down hard into her throat, tasting her blood as it filled his mouth. It was all it took to bring him over the edge once more, for his cock to empty deep and his heart to fill with love of her.

When she turned off the water, he held her still. There was something so tender about holding the person he loved after having sex that he'd never noticed before. Elijah thought that having a mate at any time was about all a man could ask for in the world. Reaching for a towel when she shivered, he dried her off, then himself, and thought of all the things that he wanted to do with her.

"I think I'm going to hire a crew to work for me." She turned to him, the towel wrapped around her beautiful body, and asked him why. "So I can spend more time being with you. I know that sounds sort of sappy. I guess it is, but I miss being with you all day."

"I'm not sure that's a good idea." He tried not to be hurt, but when she grinned at him, he felt his heart mend just a little. "We'd never leave this room if you didn't need to go to work at some point. And I'd have to close up my shop, and I'd really hate to do that as well. As it is now, I can barely go all day without wanting to hunt you down and jump your bones."

"Hey, whenever the mood strikes, I think you should hunt until you find me." She leaned against the wall and smiled at him. "I miss doing the things that you're doing with Sterl."

"Sterl needs me." He nodded, and he knew that too. But it didn't make him any less jealous of him. "And when the baby comes, you're going to have to help me learn how to be a good parent. I have no idea how that works."

"I'm positive that you're going to be wonderful at it." He looked down at her flat belly. "I can't wait to see you large with our child. To see it move and feel it there."

"I'm afraid." He wanted to tell her that she'd be great with the baby, but she continued. "I have gone without for so long. I know that you have money and so do I. Why you won't let me put the check in your account is beyond me. But I worry that we'll be broke, or someone will come and take the house from us. And the car. I love having transportation and pretty clothing. Warm boots when I want them too."

"I want you to have all of that." She nodded, and he stood in front of her. "I swear, Noelle, that we don't have to worry about money. I've done well for myself, and I have more than enough to keep you in pretty things and warm boots."

"Don't make fun of me." He kissed her and said that he wasn't. "I see others struggling with money. I know this plant is going to help a great many people, but some of them it can't. And if you quit your job, how will I help them?"

"I'm not sure what you mean." She moved into their bedroom, and he waited. There was something there and he was almost afraid to find out what it was. "Noelle, do you have a plan for me to work on?"

"I bought a loom. And a quilter. Do you know what those are?" He said that he knew but had no idea how to work them. "I want learn how to use them, learn them enough that I can show you if you want. I was thinking I'd like to teach the people at the nursing home how to use them as well. Some may already know, but I think it will give them a sense of purpose that they don't have now."

He had no idea why that had anything to do with him quitting his job, but pulled on his clothing while she got around to it. She told him of the material that she'd gotten for almost nothing, the sewing notions as well. And when she was fully dressed, she turned to him.

"If you're here, with me, I won't go anywhere. I won't want to." He started to tell her he was confused when it hit him. "There are so many things that I want to do."

"You're afraid that if I'm out of work, I'll be making demands on your time and you won't want to go to work. Honey, I'd never do that to you. Well, I would be making demands on your pretty body, but not to the point where you couldn't do the things that are important to you." She looked up at him, and he was positive that she wasn't sure about it. "I promise you this...I will work every day if you promise me that when the urge hits you to jump my bones, you'll come and do it. And if I want to chase you around your store, you'll let me do that as well."

"You're not mad." Actually, he was very proud of her but only shook his head. "You don't have to work all day, just enough that I can get this started. I need to do this."

"Well, of course you do. I love it. You're going to be a big hit at the nursing home too. Mrs. Baker, the lady with the B&B? She is in charge of the activities there. Mom helps her sometimes. I bet she'd love to get you started."

She was nearly dancing down the stairs. He was going to work every day and leave her to her job because she didn't want him around, and Elijah was happy as he'd ever been. He revised his earlier thought. Having a mate was the best thing a man could hope for in the universe.

CHAPTER 13

She was here. All he could focus on was that Helenia was here. Trent moved to stand beside his brothers and sat down. They were all their wolves for this, and he prayed to God this worked. As she stood there, her entire demeanor terrifying, he kept his mind focused on one thing. This was going to work.

"Noah, I want my alpha." Noah was there, but in the shadows. He'd only come out when it was necessary. And he said if it was necessary for them to run for cover, it was going to be bad. She looked at them, all eight of them, standing there. Even his dad and grandda had joined them. "Which one of you is the one that I killed for?"

"You can't tell, Helenia? Well, that's really too bad. I thought—well, I guess we all thought—that you'd be able to tell which one of these men you planned to murder." Myra looked at them, then back at Helenia as she continued to taunt her. "Come now, there is only one of them that you marked, correct? You're supposed to be this great and powerful...whatever you are. Pick him out and we'll be done with this."

"I'm more powerful than you will ever be." Trent had been worried about that as well, the difference in power between the two women. But when Chris Bentley had shown up with her mate and his family, he'd felt a little better. They had lined up behind Helenia and were now waiting for the word to attack. "Where is my alpha? He and I will be the greatest threat to mankind that they have ever known."

"Oh, come now. You really think that you're going to take over the world? With a wolf? I mean they are strong—and this particular family is one of the strongest I've ever had the pleasure of working with—but all of mankind?" Myra looked at him again and winked, this time before looking at the she-devil in front of them. "I'm thinking that you've lost something with him, haven't you? More than what Noah and I took from him. You've lost...well, you're not as strong as you once thought you were, are you, Helenia?"

"I don't know what you're talking about." But he heard it in her voice. Her uncertainty. "I'm going to take him with me or kill them all. Tell me which one is mine."

"None of them are yours." The hardiness of her voice was in direct contrast to the comical way that Myra was dressed today. "You will not take any of them."

Her outfit—because that's what he'd begun calling her outlandish clothing—was all camo. Even her hair was greens, browns, and black. There were even dark smudges under her eyes and along her cheeks. He's asked Joe once if she thought the woman's panties as well as bra changed with her clothing, and they'd laughed for nearly an hour trying to outdo one another as to what color she wore with each outfit.

When Helenia moved toward them, Trent stood up with the rest of them. Sterl was right beside him, and he could feel his fear. This was going to be good for his brother if things turned out the way they had planned. If not...well, he was pretty sure that they'd all be dust if it didn't. Immortal or not, it was going to be difficult to live through the kind of power this woman had on her worst days.

"Come to me, alpha. You belong to me." None of them moved and Myra laughed. Helenia turned to her, the anger she felt toward the witch palatable. "What do you think you're even doing here? This is no concern of yours. Leave before I kill you as well."

That was the cue, the one that they'd hoped for. Chris Bentley came out of the house and stood at Myra's side. When she pulled out a list and began reading the names from it, Sterl sat back down, as did the rest of his family.

"Helenia, I'm Chris, the Grand Witch of all witches. Catchy title, don't you think?" Trent watched both women as Chris continued. "You've killed a few witches in your lifetime. I'm here to collect on their debt."

"So? I don't owe you anything. Not for killing for power. It was necessary to strengthen myself. Not that I needed all that much more. When I was created, I was already more powerful than anyone." Chris nodded. "You have no stand here either. Be gone. I have business to conduct and you are in my way."

"Actually, I do have business with you. A lot of it, as a matter of fact. You killed witches, as I have pointed out. And while some of them you received power from, others you did not take what should have rightfully been yours." Helenia said nothing. "And as such, it is my duty to take a percentage of what you have now in payment for the family. I was thinking one quarter of a percent of what you have now. For each of them."

"So you think to charge me for not taking the power of a witch that I killed? No. I won't allow it." Chris only smiled at her. "You cannot take what does not belong to you. I won this magic by rights of your own laws."

"So you did. But you did murder others for no other reason than to kill them. That is against all bylaws, even the ones that you rarely follow of your own kind. And as such, it is well within my power to take it back. One quarter of a percent for each of them."

"There are no others like me. I am the first, the strongest." Chris said nothing. "How many are you talking about? There cannot be that many that you needed to come here, at this time, to take it from me. I have things to do, and as I have pointed out, you are in my way."

"You'll be dead soon enough, and I want to finish this." Helenia laughed. "You don't believe me? Well, I suppose you can do that should you want. But I'm taking what is rightfully the family's. Now."

Helenia staggered to her knees. Then when it was apparent that she was going to be sick too, she lay down, holding her body much like one of them did when they were shot with silver. As she lay there, Chris turned to Trent.

"When she is gone, you will need to be prepared for what will come to you." He asked her what that would be. "Everything minus what share I will receive. Your family will...I'm not sure what it will do to you as a wolf, but it might be painful for a few minutes." She looked at Sterl then. "I should like to advise you on something. Strike quickly and hard. And when you have done so, back away. Do not leave, but back away from her."

As one the leap of panthers turned and left for the woods. Chris moved to her car, but Myra stayed with them. Trent wasn't sure what was going to happen now, but he knew that whatever it was, Sterl had to do it. He looked at his brother and nodded.

The shift was quick. When he pulled on his pants that had been just behind them all, he moved forward and kicked Helenia in the face, causing her nose to bleed. As soon as he did, he stumbled back and fell to the ground. Before Trent could go to his aid, the ground shook beneath them.

The...he supposed the being that seemed to come up from the swollen ground looked like every nightmare he'd ever had. He was pretty sure that he'd think about this thing more so now that he'd seen him. But almost as soon as he was ready to turn and have his family run, the being turned into a man, complete with a suit and tie. Then he turned to Trent.

"If you would be so kind as to turn to yourself, I would be appreciative. I have made myself...easier, I guess, for you to see. If you would be so kind, I will finish this." Trent wasn't sure what he was to do, but let his wolf go and stood before the man. He was dressed too, in the jeans and tee he'd had on before this started. "Ah, not the wolf I was looking to find. I'm looking for the one that she called her own."

"That would be me. But I belong to no one." Trent and the others, all men, moved to stand beside Sterl as he continued. "I hurt her first. She has to leave. I want you all gone from here now."

~~~

Elijah stood by Sterl and the rest of them, ready to do whatever was necessary to keep them all alive. When Joe and Noelle, along with his grandmother and mom, came out to stand with them, Elijah took Noelle's hand and held it tightly in his. Whatever happened now, he was ready to go out with the people he loved. The man looked at him.

"You have it right." Elijah said nothing, but he seemed to be okay with that. "I am Richard. Not a very sexy name for a demon, but there you have it. I have come because you have injured someone that I created. Helenia."

"She hurt my brother more than he did her. You have no idea what sort of suffering he's had to endure because she decided that she wanted him to father her minions." Richard looked down at Helenia as Elijah continued. "If you want to take us on because of this, you're going to regret it."

"I already do. But not what has happened today." He snapped his fingers, and Helenia stood up. "A fine creature, don't you think? When her parents summoned me all those millennia ago, I thought it would be simple. Help them create a child to give their magic too. But alas, they tricked me. Not only did they summon me for a child that had been born of hatred and lust, but they wanted for her things that were not of this world and should never have been. But I was trapped and had to comply. The only thing I was able to do was take them, which has worked out well for me, and to put a stipulation on her body. She knew of this from the very beginning. I'm sorry that it has taken so long for it to happen."

"Wait a minute. You helped them make her this way? Then you regretted it? You know that makes no sense whatsoever. Why not just kill her from the start and be done with it?" Helenia started to leap at them, but with another snap of his fingers, she was brought to the ground again. "She's mad."

"She is at that. Power and hunger can do that to someone." He sat down on a chair that had not been there before. "You are Elijah, are you not? And your pack master is Trent."

When he nodded, everyone but him, Trent and Sterl disappeared, including Helenia. "They are unharmed and they are safe, and when we are finished here, I will return them to this ground. But I should like to speak to the three of you for now, to explain what happened. I should hope that…well, if what I tell you is spread about, I will return and bring a hell down on you that you will never survive, immortal or not. Have a seat."

Looking around, Elijah saw that they each now had a chair like the one that Richard was sitting in. When Trent sat down, Elijah and Sterl followed suit. A scantily dressed woman brought them drinks, which they all declined. Richard assured them that there was nothing in them that would harm them.

"If it's all the same to you, I'd just as soon get this finished. She was injured, and from what we were told, she was to be taken from this world." Richard nodded at Trent. "And yet here you are making small talk as if this thing you made didn't try to kill my brother. She also murdered some very nice people because they were in her way."

"I need to tell you a story. It's important that you understand it all before we can complete this ritual. And it is one. Without it, she or someone like her may return." Trent nodded. "Thank you. Her parents were a witch and a vampire. Neither of them were in love…I'm not even sure they were mates. But they bargained for a child, one that I could give them in exchange for the opportunity to take them when they were no longer useful to her. I should have been more careful in my agreeing with them. But as I said, they trapped me. I shan't tell you how, but in the end, it was them that suffered the greatest for their deeds." Sterl asked if he had been the one that had given her the magic. "Some, not all. The earth cradled her into its power, a dark black place that only a few can enter and live. When she was born, I killed her parents, took them with me, and put her into the earth to mature and grow. She was dead by then, the dagger

171

that I used more powerful than any other forged then or since."

Richard pulled it out of the air and it moved to Elijah's hands. Elijah wasn't sure why he had it, but he put it on the ground beside him, not wanting to touch something so vile. Richard laughed at him.

"You should have died when it touched your flesh. I would not have allowed you to die, but since you have lived, the dagger is now yours. It will no longer be of any use to me." Elijah told him he didn't want it. "I did not give you the dagger, my young pup, it came to you. I thought perhaps it would have gone to the injured one, but it picked you. It is your magic now."

"As I said, I don't want it." Neither the knife nor the man moved. "What is it you're stalling for? Why haven't you left us and taken her with you?"

"I will, in good time." Richard looked at Trent. "You are a good pack master. I have, over the decades, seen what you have become. Not just you, but your family. You see, I knew that someday we'd meet and that one of you would be hurt by her. It was the way things fell in place. It would never have been your death, as she planned, but things have to play out or nothing can be solved. You understand that more than most, I think."

"So you knew all along that she was going to try and take my brother?" Richard nodded and said that he was right. "She's a monster. And so are you for making her."

"You are right on both points." Richard looked around, then back at them. "The dagger was made to kill. That's important to know. And the one that touched it, or in this case, the one that it chose, must kill Helenia. I thought, as I said before, that it would have been either Trent or Sterling."

"Gladly." But before Elijah could say anything else, like bring the bitch back so I can do it, the demon spoke again.

"To kill her you must first know how to do it. And where to stick the blade. Do you know her story? Where she was first stabbed with it?" Elijah said it had been her heart. "Correct. But she no longer has a heart. When she was turned into what she is, the heart in her chest, along with her blood, spilled upon the ground to nourish her. You must stab the place where it is."

"I don't understand." Richard nodded as if he knew he was going to say that. "You're saying that I have to find this black place, stab this dagger that should have killed me into it, and then she'll be dead."

"Yes." But before he could ask him how that was possible, Sterl put his hand on his arm to still him. Richard looked at him, directly at Sterl, when he spoke. "You do know that he must do this for you, do you not?"

"I do." Sterling stood up and Elijah had a feeling that Sterl was going to tell him he had to stab him. Sterl turned to him and smiled. "The earth. She's poisoned the earth where she was."

They all looked at the ground where Sterl had kicked her. The ground was black, and a boiling sort of tar-like substance was popping its liquid as it grew. It was all Elijah could do to pull his eyes away from the ground that had been poisoned.

"She did this?" Richard nodded. "And you want me to stab this dagger into that mess? What will it do?"

"First, it will cure the ground. I've never liked the way the earth can spew forth its troubles like this, but I am not in charge of such things. But you must be careful of the poison. Secondly, it will end Helenia for you all. And me as well. She will belong to me for longer than she was a creature of this plane."

Elijah was ready to do anything, but he knew there was a catch. "What do I lose when I do this?" Richard asked him what he meant. "You say this, that I'm to kill her for all of mankind. That it'll end her life and our suffering here. You'll gain her as whatever you have prearranged for her. Yet I think there is more to this than you just being a nice demon and telling me how to do this."

"So untrusting." Richard spoke to Trent. "Is all of your family this way? So ready to think that I could not be doing this because I'm, as he called me, a nice demon?"

"Are you?" Richard laughed and told Trent that he was far from it. "Then I think that Elijah is right. You need something more. Or something is going to hurt us in some way for doing this for you. What is it that you're going to gain, exactly? As well as what is going to happen to us should Elijah take the knife to the ground?"

Elijah felt the first touch to his mind and waited. Noah laughed then. It was so full of humor that he had to smile. And when he spoke, Elijah was sure that the man was having a hard time holding his mirth about something.

You have frustrated him badly, my friend. And you are right to question him. He does know something that he's not telling you. Elijah asked him what it was. *I don't know. Not yet at any rate. Myra is beside herself for not realizing that he'd take her away from your group. But I can be there, and while he might know it, he cannot touch me.*

Do I want to know why? Noah assured him he'd tell him later. *Should I do as he asks then? I'd really like to get this shit over and done with. I want to have fun with my mate. Raise my child in a place where this she bitch shit hole isn't breathing down my neck every time I take him out to swing on the swing. Nor having a demon ready to pop in whenever he has a favor to ask of me.*

That's it. He waited for Noah to explain but again, he was laughing. *Oh my, Elijah, you are brilliant. Yes, tell him that is what you want in agreement for doing his job. A tree that will grow long after you have left this earth, and that will have many seedlings that will grow just as strong and healthy.*

But I'm an immortal, right? Noah assured him that he was. *Then I don't understand why.... You know what? I don't care. And this will work? This will end it so that we're all happy?*

Happy might be a term that I'd not use with the demon, but he will comply. Tell him like I said, you want a tree of oak that will live long after you have left this earth, and that its seedlings will be just as healthy. Do it now while I watch his face. Elijah told him he was nuts. *I am, but this will work.*

"All right, I'll do this but I want something in return. I mean, this is benefiting you, so I'd like some reassurances. For my own peace of mind. And if you don't follow it, I'll take the dagger and destroy it. If I can." Richard nodded and stood up when the rest of them did. "I want you to put an oak tree here where I cure the earth. I want it to be here, strong and steady, long after I leave this earth. As well as its seedlings...all of them must be as strong as this one, and healthy."

Elijah wasn't sure he was going to do it. Anger was evident on his face, but while he was pissed off, he never took his anger out on them. When he laughed, hard and hearty, Elijah wasn't sure what to think. Then Richard bowed before them.

"As you wish. A mighty oak to grow in the place where once there was death and poison. Children of such tree to propagate and make more of the same. It will only die, not from disease nor another other element, but a cut to the body that would fell it. The same with the others. Is this what you want?" Noah told him to say yes it was. "Good, then you shall have it. Take the dagger, young pup, and cure your earth, and I will take Helenia from this place to my own."

"Thank you." He wasn't sure if he should shake the demon's hand or not, but put it out for him to take should he want. When he gripped his thick hand around his, Elijah felt the power of it all the way to his toes and then back up again. "You are a man of your word. And I of mine."

Taking the dagger into his hand, Elijah asked Noah if he was going to be all right. *You will be wonderfully fine. As will your family, all of them.*

The dagger felt warm in his hand, the power of it, because there was little doubt to Elijah that it was power that hummed up his arm. And when he plunged it into the earth, the dark liquid screamed and the ground once again trembled. As he was ready to ask Noah if he had done it right, he was thrown back, his body lifted up and tossed away from the area like he'd been nothing more than a leaf in the wind. Then there was nothingness.

CHAPTER 14

Noelle was going to kill someone. She really didn't care who it was at this point, but she wanted someone to pay. She glared at Trent when he laughed. Again.

"You can't make him wake up by being all pissed off. Maybe, as I have suggested several times now, you should go down to the kitchen and get you something to eat. The baby needs it." She huffed. "And that won't work either. You're supposed to be in awe of me, not mean."

"You're a prick. And he's been out for three days. I want him to wake up now. The rest of you got up quickly." She'd never been so terrified in her life when the door she'd been trying to open for twenty minutes suddenly did as she wanted and tossed her back on her ass. Then something—she was still trying to get that answer from someone—had hit her. Hard. "I'm supposed to go and talk to Howard today. And I'm meeting Ron and Daniel for lunch afterwards."

"I can stay here with him." She told Trent she wanted Elijah to go with her. "I'm not sure that's going to be possible. He's still resting."

If she could have gotten away with it, Noelle was sure she could have easily murdered Trent right where he sat. She glanced at Elijah again and wondered what he'd think about her being in prison.

"He will be fine." She asked Trent how he knew. "Because the rest of us are. And he saved us all by doing what he did. I'm still not sure about the tree, but I guess he'll explain it to us when he wakes up."

"Noah told him to ask for it. He told me yesterday that it had been Elijah's idea to have a tree to swing his children on. When I asked him what that had to do with the earth, he told me that the oak has a deep root, much like the one in his family. That we get our strength much like the tree does from the earth. Asking Richard for the oak and to keep it safe for all of us said to him that we were going to be here for a good long time, long enough to make sure that we hold him to his promise. I guess even with him being a demon like he is, he is a man of his word." Noelle thought of something else that Noah had told her. "He knew who he was. Noah knows Richard. Not as a demon, but I guess they ran into each other many years ago and Noah knew what he was. I guess few can recognize a demon when they see them. Noah did."

"I heard him telling Grandda that there was a connection between the two of them, and that Richard vowed never to hurt such a creature as Noah. I wonder if that is the reason." Noelle said she wasn't sure but supposed it could be. "Noelle, I promise you, I can hear Elijah's heart beating normally, as well as his breathing is fine. He will wake when he wakes."

She knew, deep in her heart, that he was going to be all right. But that didn't lessen the fact that she wanted him awake, holding her in his arms, loving her.

"I talked to Sterl yesterday. He said that he's never felt better. I guess he's enjoying his painting too. And I'm helping him find a staff. Alta said that she can't keep picking up after him and feeding him well too. I think he's eating better as well." Trent nodded, and she stood up to walk to the window. "Have you messed with the power that we got? I mean, even to see what we can do?"

"Some. When we shift, we're dressed as we were before we changed. I can bring things to me with just a thought. Also, I have this ability to read the mind of some of the pack...not all, but a few. Mostly it's when they're hiding something, like they've no money for a bill or that they're without food. Joe and the others can as well. It's come in handy when we go to see people around the pack land." She nodded. "What is it you have figured out?"

"I can feel my child. Not just when it moves, but hear it talking to me. It's strange to feel...I can feel that I'm having twins too. A boy and a girl. I've not told anyone but you, so if you could just not say anything for a few more weeks, I'd appreciate it." Noelle watched the oak sway in the yard. There was a big fully grown one in each of their yards, even the cabin in the woods that Trent and Joe stayed at sometimes. "Yesterday when I took a walk in the yard, a sapling fell from the tree. Not a seed, but a sapling. When I took it in the house to see to it, I had the feeling that it was to be planted near the pond, and that your grandma was to help me do it."

"She told me that you and her planted one of the trees. Do you know why?" She nodded. "If you know that she's to pass and that you wanted to have this tree, please don't. I love her too much to let her go now that she's back here."

"No, nothing like that. But did she tell you what she told me when we were finished?" Trent said that he wasn't sure what she meant. "When we had the tree in the soil, we stood back and watched as new branches formed over it and leaves began to uncurl. Jasmine took my hand in hers and told me that when she'd been younger, a man had come to their land and had been upset that some of his sheep had been killed. He must have guessed what they were, she told me, and he accused your grandda of killing them. The man said he was going to hang Trent Senior from the tree and had put a rope around him to do so. She said that she'd not been able to shift, she'd been so afraid that he'd kill them both. Jasmine was carrying your dad at the time. But he only got your grandda in the tree when it broke. The branch fell and hit the man on the head and killed him."

"I'd heard that before. When I was a child. Grandda said that since he'd not shifted to heal the numerous wounds that the man had caused, the law back then had ruled it self-defense and that there was never any mention of it again. Even his wife, the other man's, had said that her husband hadn't been right in the head for some time. Something about poor whisky." She continued to watch the tree. "They buried him under a tree. I'm betting it was an oak."

"It was." Turning back to Trent, she could see the confusion on his face. She was all right with that there; she'd been feeling a great deal of that herself. "I'd like to take a nap. With Elijah. If you'd just go away, I'd be really happy."

"Do you dislike me, Noelle?" She asked him why he'd ask her that. "I'm not sure. But lately, since we dealt with Richard and Helenia, I've had the feeling that you'd rather I wasn't around. Not just here, but at all. Why is that?"

"You should have taken the dagger." He said nothing, but stared at her. "Why was he the one that had to do this? Why didn't you do it if you're his leader or whatever you are to him? He's suffering because you didn't protect him."

Trent didn't move from the chair. Her heart hurt now for saying aloud what she'd been thinking for too long. When he did stand, she had a feeling that he was pissed. And when he stood in front of her, she could see his wolf as he moved along his face, and he was there in his eyes.

"Every moment of each day that he lays there, I wonder the same thing. I wonder why the dagger went to him and not me. Why he was the one that was to cure the earth and not me. And why he got the brunt of whatever happened and not me." She watched as tears rolled down his face, the same as they did on hers. "You think that it was my grand plan to get him hurt? It wasn't. I have no idea what happened to him that day, not a clue. But in a heartbeat, I'd gladly trade him places."

"I need him." Trent said that he did as well. "He's all I have in the world. The only person who has ever loved me, made me feel secure. And now he won't wake up for me. I need him."

"I'm sorry." Trent pulled her into his arms and held her tightly. Noelle felt the love then, the overwhelming sorrow coming from Trent. And when she felt herself go weak with the pain of all this, he picked her up and laid her beside Elijah. "I'm so very sorry, Noelle. But I promise you that he'll wake, and when he does, he'll tell you what both Sterl and I did. That we had nothing to do with what happened out there. That he was the one that the dagger chose, not me."

"I want him awake, Trent. I want to feel his arms around me. His love for me. I'm so afraid." He said that he was as well. "What if he never wakes up? What will happen to me and his children?"

"We will care for you as he would have. Love them and tell them about their daddy every day, and show them all the pictures that we have. But you won't have to worry about this happening. He's going to be fine. You have to believe that." She nodded, still hurt. "Sleep, love. Just hold him in your arms and sleep with him. You've not been resting well. Okay?"

As she was rolled to her side and a blanket laid over them both, all she could think about was her children, hers and Elijah's, and what she was going to do if he left her like this. Closing her eyes, she felt the weight of the world on her shoulders, the sadness of being alone and all the other emotions that she knew were right there on the sidelines just waiting to make themselves known to her.

Just as she was ready to get up and pace again, she saw Noah. When he touched his fingers to her forehead and said "Sleep," there was nothing she could do but fall into the deep abyss he seemed to throw her into.

~~~

Every part of him was warm, almost hot. Elijah wanted to toss off the heavy blanket over him and reached out to do so when he touched his fingers to her skin. He knew that it was Noelle, knew the feel of her flesh as he did his own. Rolling to his back carefully, he looked down at her sleeping face.

"Do not wake her just yet." He looked at the chair next to his bed and saw Noah sitting there with the stupid envelope on his lap. "She's not been well, trying her best to will you to get better and wake up for her. I think she even told Trent to go away at some point."

"Is she all right?" Noah said she was all right now that he'd put her to sleep for a few hours. "How long have I been here?"

"Just a little over three days. I would have thought longer, but I'm glad you're awake now so I can speak to you. Helenia is gone." Elijah said he'd hoped so. "Yes, well, she's not dead, though I would bet she wishes that she was. Helenia is the fuck bitch for Richard and any other creature he wishes to share her with. I'm thinking that Helenia will receive the kind of hell that she deserves. Thanks to you."

"I only did what you told me to do." Noah nodded and smiled. "Was there a reason for the tree? I mean, you were so excited about it."

"Oaks are something that few know can kill a demon. Tossing an acorn at one will have them running in the opposite direction, despite their magic. And not just the wood, but every part of it. And the young saplings, they're the most toxic of all. If you capture a demon, build a box from an oak and he'll never be able to get out of it once you put him inside." Elijah asked him how that was to happen. "I never figured that out either, but I do know that they're deathly afraid of the mighty oak tree."

"And when I asked for it, I was telling him what? Telling him that I meant business, or that I knew about the oak and what it would do to him?" Noah laughed and said he hoped he thought of both. "Do you think he knows you're the one who told me that?"

"I'm sure of it. As I mentioned, few know much about demons and what it takes to harm one." Elijah looked down at Noelle and Noah cleared his throat. "You must tell her that you were the one to do this because of the dagger. She blames your brother for not saving you."

"I'll talk to her. She was there, just before I was taken under. I could feel her fear." Noah nodded. "Was there something else? Something that I should know right now?"

"Yes. The magic has been given to all of you. Including your grandparents and parents. Even I got a little. Myra said that Chris did that for all of you to be around for a long while. She said that she'd be back if you had any questions." Elijah nodded. "Noelle got a good deal more because of her breeding."

"You mean our child got some of it too." Noah nodded. "Why do I have the feeling that you're not telling me it all? And that when the time comes, you're going to be laughing your ass off when I figure it out?"

"I'm a jolly man like that, I guess." He stood up. "No one was harmed in this family. All of you, as I said, have a bit of it. You and Sterling, you both got the bulk of it. And so you know, he's going to be just fine now. Better, as a matter of fact."

"Good. If anyone deserves it, he does. He's been through a lot." Noah nodded. "Now, if there is nothing else pressing, I'd very much like to wake my mate and make love to her for a few hours. And if it's all the same to you, I'd rather you weren't here."

"I understand completely." Noah moved to the door and paused before turning. "Noelle still hasn't opened her settlement from her father. You should do that soon. There are things there that are going to make her very happy. You too."

"Is it more magic?" Noah said there was some, but not as much as they'd gotten from Helenia. He told him it was going to make them very rich, richer than they were at present. "Then it can wait. I need to be with Noelle now and then we'll take care of it. All right?"

When Noah left them, laughing, Elijah tried to decide the best way to wake Noelle. All sorts of delightful things came to mind and he got out of the bed. Stripping down to his bare skin, he let his wolf take him. Time for them both to have a little fun.

As he was pulling the blanket off her, she rolled to her back. He was glad to find her naked and warm too. Elijah hadn't thought of her position on the bed when his wolf had come to him. Leaping up on the bed, he sat between her legs and nudged her legs wider open with his nose. Her scent was soft, sweet smelling in her slumber. As soon as he licked her, he was surprised at how quickly she went from nothing to aroused. Christ, she was going to kill them both one of these days, he knew it. Lying down, his wolf licked her again, and when she moaned, he moved closer to feast on her more.

She tasted different to him. Not just the fact that she was carrying his child now, but there was something more, a hint of magic that he and his wolf could taste. Sliding his tongue deep into her pussy had her rolling her hips up to meet him, and Elijah knew it was only a matter of time before she woke screaming his name. The feel of her fingers curling into his fur had him watching her, and when she sat up, she fell over the edge as he took her juices into his body. His wolf growled low when his fur was pulled.

Come for us again, baby. We need more of you. She lay back on the bed, spreading her legs wide for them. His wolf moved closer, taking his time now with bringing her as much pleasure as he could give his mate. And when she cupped her breasts, pulling on the tight nubs there, he was hungry for a taste of her as well. When his wolf sat up and threw back his head to howl, every part of him felt it. And so did Noelle.

As soon as he was released, his wolf letting him have his mate, Elijah lifted her up to this mouth and devoured her, ate not just of her pussy but her thighs and hips, her navel as well as her ass. There wasn't a part of her that he didn't want a taste of, and when she cried out again that she was coming, he spread her nether lips open and watched as the cream flowed from her.

"Please, Elijah, I need to feel you inside of me." He moved up her then, slowly, nipping and tasting her flesh as he went. Her breasts were suckled, her nipples feasted upon.

Even her throat felt his mouth, his teeth as he made his way to her mouth. And kissing her, sliding his tongue over hers, Elijah knew a new kind of pleasure. Her hunger matched his own.

Sliding into her heat, he paused. She was tight, her body milking his as he was poised to fill her completely. And when she wrapped her arms around his shoulders, her legs over his hips, Elijah watched her face as he made love her to her slowly, pulling back out only to fill her again and again.

"I love you." She said that she loved him as well, with a catch in her voice that made him smile. "I can never get enough of you. I don't think I even want to try."

"Take me, Elijah, please." This time when he moved into her, he slammed forward. It took her breath away and his too. He fucked her hard now, each stroke a little harder, and each time he slid to his tip, he held her closer to him. When she dug her nails into his back, her nails cutting deeply, Elijah found her pounding pulse and bit down over it. Her second scream of release had his wolf snarling at him to take her again.

Pounding her now, taking her up and over several times as he drank deeply from her, he felt the moment that he was ready, that his cock and balls were full now to release. Lifting his mouth from her throat, he let his beast roll over him as he came hard and completely. Then he came again, then again as his body felt the need to fill her.

As he dropped down, his body no less spent than he felt like she was, he pulled her atop him and held her to him as his heart slowed and his mind didn't feel like it was running too fast. She was limp over him, and he used the last of his strength to pull the blanket over them both when she shivered. Elijah was sure that he was going to die now, that he'd peaked too soon. When she lifted her head up and looked down at him, he didn't even have any energy left to smile at her.

"You've killed me." Her giggle had him looking at her with one eye closed. "I'm not kidding. I think you've drained me to the very end, and then for good measure, you sucked all my good intentions out as well."

"What sort of good intentions did you have, waking me with your wolf eating me for his breakfast?" Well, he thought, she did have him there. "I've been really worried about you. Trent said you'd be all right, but I didn't believe him."

"He was worried as well. I think when the dagger came to me instead of him, he was ready to jerk it from me and do what needed to be done." She laid her head down, not saying anything. "Trent would have done it if he could have."

"Did you talk to him then? To Trent when you woke up?" He told her he had not, not yet. "I was mad at him before he left here today. I think I might have hurt his feelings."

"Just talk to him. He's not mad at you." At least he'd better not be. "Have you spoken to Sterl? I mean, since I've been sleeping my life away?"

"Yes. He's been in and out, all of them have. But he's been staying here too. Trent came in too every day, but your grandparents and Sterl have been staying here with me at night." He nodded. "I really like Jasmine."

"Jasmine? Oh, Grandma. I forgot...well, I never think of her as having a first name. She's always been just 'Grandma' to me." He held Noelle, stroking her back with his fingers now that his strength was returning. "Grandma said that they wanted to hang around until the baby is born. She wants to knit things for it."

"Them." He asked her what she meant around a yawn that seemed to make him feel better. "We're having twins. A boy and a girl."

"What?" When she didn't answer him right away, he rolled her to her back and leaned over her. "Twins? You're having twins?"

"No, *we're* having twins." She took his hand down to her flat belly and put it over it. "Listen to them. You can hear them too, I bet."

Holding his breath, he felt her belly, the warmth of it under his hand. And when he heard the small sound, more like a chirping than a voice, he knew immediately that it was his daughter. The second sound, his son, was there too. Elijah kissed Noelle without taking his hand from his children and the connection he had there.

"I told Trent, I mean about the babies, and he promised not to tell anyone else." Elijah nodded, not caring who knew that he was going to have twins, one of each. "I thought it would be more fun for us to tell your parents and grandparents."

Elijah jumped from the bed and began searching for his clothing. A sock was under the bed; his pants were over the back of the chair. When Noelle laughed and asked him what he was doing, he told her getting ready to see his family.

"I'm pretty sure that we can wait for a little while. I mean, we have nine months." Elijah was so let down that he felt himself pouting. "Oh all right, you big baby, we'll tell them, but you need to shower. You smell of burnt dog."

"Will you join me?" He wiggled his brows at her and smiled when she laughed. "All right, I'll shower alone. In the big bathroom all by myself."

She was laughing when he turned on the water and looked in the mirror. The man staring back at him looked so much different than he thought he should. Elijah felt...older. Then he realized that wasn't it...he felt like his mind was stronger, along with his body. Like he'd been packed with a great deal of information in a short amount of time. As he stood there wondering where that thought came from, he saw the mark on his shoulder. It was a small bejeweled dagger.

Trying not to freak the fuck out any more than he was, he reached for Noah. He'd woken him, for which Elijah was sorry, but he needed to know what this meant. The dagger looked just like the one that had come to him.

It's saying that you survived a demon. Richard, as a matter of fact. And so you know, I spoke to him last night...well, the day before yesterday now, and he said that while you might be marked, he wasn't sure, he would not be able to find you. You and the rest of the Calhouns are untouchable to him and his kind. Elijah asked him what that meant. *That no demon, or any product of a demon, can harm you. That you are as safe from them and their spells as anyone has ever been. That would include any and all children you take into your hearts too.*

You mean adopted. Noah said that was what he figured, but hadn't thought to ask. *I'm not sure what to think about this. I mean, does Trent or the rest of them know?*

No. I figured if you wanted them to know, that you'd tell them. He could almost feel the other man's exhaustion. *I must rest, my good friend. I have had a long day and a longer night. If that is all, I can rest and see you on the sunset.*

Yes, that's fine. I'm sure that I'll have a thousand and one questions by then. The connection closed with laughter from Noah. Elijah took his shower and dressed. Really, clothing just appeared on him when he thought of them. That was the first question he was going to ask the man about.

CHAPTER 15

Noelle was as nervous as she'd ever been about anything. Seeing her stepbrothers today, then going to see her stepfather, was something that she'd never dreamed would happen. Not like this at any rate. They were going to see Howard, and she was going to tell him what she thought of him. Then he was going to prison upstate to await his trial. It was too much, and she tried to think of something else. The stupid envelope.

It had been full. Not just full, but too many things had been in the envelope for its size. The legal sized envelope had had fifty stacks of one hundred dollar bills, and deeds to several properties and houses that were all in hers and Elijah's names. There were also the directions to three safety deposit boxes in the local bank that they were going to look into after this. The money alone had made her sick to her stomach. To have so much money, five hundred thousand dollars in cash, had been a bit more than she'd ever dreamed of. Noelle was richer than she could ever have imagined she'd ever be.

When the limo pulled up in front of the jail house, she grabbed Elijah's hand and held him tighter to her. Her belly was protesting the stress, and she was afraid that the men coming to see her would tell her to fuck off, as they had plenty of times in her past.

"Just breathe. I have it on good authority that they're just as nervous as you are. And you've got me. Think how alone they're feeling about now." She had, a great deal over the last few hours. "Come on now, go tell them how glad you are to see them."

Moving forward, she was standing nearby when they both got out of the car and it moved down the street. Both of them had lost a great deal of weight over the last few weeks since she'd seen them, and their clothing was starting to look baggy. Ron hugged her, something that he'd never done in all her life. Then Daniel did. He held her for a few minutes before he stepped back.

"We were afraid that you'd not show." She nodded, too emotionally upset to speak to Daniel. "The trip here was nice...thanks for sending the car for us. To be honest, I wasn't sure how we were going to make it." Elijah shook both their hands and told them it was his pleasure. "I guess we're going to do this now. See him, I mean. I don't think he's going to be happy with any of us."

"I don't care. And to be honest with you, he can rot in hell too." Ron laughed at Noelle's words, but it was a nervous kind of sound. "After this, I'd like to take you both to lunch, then show you where you're going to be staying. The work on clearing the land, it starts Monday, so you have a few days to get things squared away."

"You've done so much for us. I mean, a lot more than we ever did for you. I can't tell you how ashamed I am for what we both did to you. I know that it's a little late, but I'm terribly sorry." She hugged Daniel again, and they made their way into the jail. Today would make a difference in all their lives. She only hoped it was in a good way.

Howard was laying on his bed. She was sure that someone would have told them that they were coming, but he lay there with no pants on and his shirt all undone. Even his feet were bare. Noelle was glad that he'd at least put his underwear on. When he turned and looked at them, she could see his anger.

"Well, if it's not the fucking cunt that put me here. And she's brought me my ungrateful bastard children. I do hope that one of you has bail money for me. I'm sick of sitting here all day with shit to do but think." Elijah told him he should have done more of that before. "Oh, and you're such a smart man that you know what I've been up to? You don't know shit. When am I getting out of here?"

"Dad, you're leaving here today." Ron looked at her with a confused look on his face.

"They didn't tell him he was leaving here? That he was going—?"

"About fucking time, if you ask me. I sure hope they got you but good for my bail, you bitch. And don't think this is going to end either. I'm going to take you for every nickel you have." Howard stood up and started pulling on his pants as he continued. "All the things that I've missed being here. But I tell you, I have me some plans. I'm going to make sure that you do right by me for all you've done to me."

"You're going to prison. Today. They're taking you up there in an hour. Ron, Daniel, and I have come to tell you that you're not going to see us again. That we're done with you." Howard looked at his sons, then at her. Noelle smiled at him. "You won't be taking anything from me again. No one is going to hire you a lawyer either. You'll be on your own."

"You let her do this to us? You let this woman tell me what she's going to do? Where the hell are your balls, boys? She got them too?" Neither of her stepbrothers said a word, but they did drop their heads. "I swear to Christ, when I get out of this shit, I'm going to start hammering into your thick empty heads what you need to do to make a woman mind you."

Ron's head shot up like he'd been yanked by his hair. "No you're not. Dad, she never did a thing to any of us. Even after what we all did to her, she and her husband are helping us find a place to stay, as well as work. Paying work." Howard snorted at Ron when he defended her. "They sent a limo for us. Made sure that we had food to eat, as well as money in our pockets."

"Give it to me." Both of them stepped back when Howard reached out for them. "You don't know what to do with money. Give it to me and I'll make sure it goes to a good cause. Namely me."

"No. I'm not going to do it. And you can't make me." Daniel looked at her. "He's been this way all our lives, hasn't he? Mean and nasty. I noticed it, but...he is just a mean, nasty man."

"You think you see a side of me that I didn't let you before? Damn it, boy, how do you think I got us fed all the time? Do you think them steaks come to you free? Well, they did, I guess, but I had to steal them for your meal. You think that was easy?" Ron backed away more, until his back was on the wall across from the cell. "Come here, Ron. Give me the cash you have on you and I'll get you something nice with it. I'm sure that we can grab us up a few nice steaks, some potatoes. You got you some nice pockets on you. We'll fill them up and keep the cash for later. For something else. Maybe I can go to the tracks with it."

"No. You're not...I'm not going to give you a thing." She knew then that Ron had believed that their father wasn't that bad. That somehow everyone, including Daniel, had misunderstood him. "You were never a good father to us. Never. You talk about those steaks, and I remember you sending us in for them, telling us how to steal them for our dinner. One time you hit me in the head when the steak I brought out wasn't right. Too veiny or something. Every penny we had, you used it for yourself. Even when Mom was alive, you took and took from her until she was dead."

"Your mom got it. She knew that we had it fine until Noelle fucked us over." Ron was shaking his head. "She did. She got me fired. Had them put those barriers up so that I'd not be able to make a living. How the hell was we supposed to survive without some help?"

"By getting a job? Or maybe being nicer to the people that wanted to help us?" Daniel looked at her as he spoke. "He would put our names on the Christmas trees all over town. But even that was a scam, a lie. He stole one of them, just snatched it off the tree and worked for two days on making it blank. Then he made copies of it, putting down all our names for presents. Then when no one was looking, he'd have us put the tags back on the tree with his phone number. Then do you know what he did? When the presents came to the house, a lot of them too, he would unwrap them, careful of the boxes, and take them back to the stores. Even sold them from the back of his car. We got nothing but a cuff in the head when we asked him what we got to keep."

"You ungrateful little fuckers. How else was I supposed to afford that television that you plopped your ass down in front of for an hour? Jesus H. Christ, has she been filling your head with all kinds of shit like that? If so, it's a good thing that you got me money to get me out of here. I'm going to teach her a few lessons she won't forget."

Noelle looked at Elijah when he growled low. His wolf was there, just waiting to get out and tear Howard apart. And he would too. So before that happened, she turned to her brothers.

"Come on. I think we've said enough and heard too much." As she started to move them out of the cell area, Howard started calling her names. Before she could get past him, however, he grabbed her arm. Without thought as to what might happen to her, she punched him in the face with her free hand and then kicked him as he went down. "You touch me again and I will tear you apart."

She was so upset that she got them out of the little room before she realized that Elijah wasn't with her. When she was ready to go and find him, he came through the door and helped them out of the building. The limo was back and waiting for them. It was then that she asked him what he'd done.

"Nothing. I swear to you. I didn't harm a hair on his head." She wanted to believe him, but he looked too satisfied. "He knows better than to mess with you now. And to never touch you again. I made him realize what could happen to him if he did."

She supposed she should have been happy with that, but she was too upset to ask any more questions. They took Ron and Daniel to the house they'd be sharing while they worked for Trent and the Calhoun family.

~~~

Scott walked around his house. He'd been all over the inside, and now he was checking out the outdoors. He needed something to do, and if he didn't get to do anything soon, he figured that he could knock down a wall or two.

Maybe even bust out a window. Anything to get his mind off the fact that he was unemployed. When he came around to the front of the house again, Grandda was there by his old beat-up truck with a huge smile on his face.

"Someone said you didn't have to clock in right now. Wanna come with me? I got a hankering to wet my fishing pole a little." Scott groaned. Fishing with Grandda usually meant long drawn-out stories that were as farfetched as they could get, and a longer period of him being stuck in a boat with him while he did it. "Come on, you and I can have some fun."

"Doubtful. You know that I can't stand fishing." Grandda smiled and got in the passenger side of his truck. "So, I guess I'm driving to my own kind of hell."

Scott walked to the driver's side and got in. He loved this old truck and the man who owned it more. As he started it up, he turned to Grandda and asked him where they were going. He said that way, as if that were real directions. Scott drove down his drive and towards town.

"We're staying with Elijah for a few days. Your grandma is looking for us a house close to the rest of you boys." Scott said there were several down the street from his house, but he was pretty sure they were huge. "I don't mind having me a bigger house. What with the great grandkids coming now, we might have us some fun with them. If your dad and mom share them."

"I'm sure you can make them do about anything you want." He nodded. "Who told you that I was out of work?"

"Saw the For Sale sign when we was house hunting. Your daddy knows too. He was the one driving us around." Scott nodded. His entire family knew now. "You get tired of telling others how to have sex? Seems to me that it comes about natural to you as breathing if you have the right person."

"I showed them how to have fun and no one get hurt while they were at it." He knew that all of his family was aware of what he'd done for a living. But he didn't want to talk about it with his grandda. "I'm going to work on the plant property when they get going. Right now I'm bored, and was about to get myself into all kinds of trouble over it. I guess your timing was perfect, even if it is just fishing."

"What if I told you that I have a deal to strike up with you? We go into a business, you and me?" Scott asked him if it dealt with fishing. "No. I know how much you hate it. But if you notice, I don't even have my stuff with me. It was just an excuse to get you all dandered up."

He hadn't noticed and said so. "What sort of business? And so you know, I might have to wait a little while before I can invest. I'm not working right now. It's not that I don't have the money, but I don't want to be scraping the bottom when nothing comes along."

"Well, you know that little girl of your brother's, Noelle? She's got herself a good head on her shoulders, and I was watching her the other day working. There's some fine pieces that she has there for sale. Pretty ones that I think she could get more for if they had them a little loving. I want to fix them up. With you." Scott didn't know what he meant. "I mean we can have us a right fine fix it up shop. I know that your daddy has some equipment in that shed of his, and we can start with that. But I was thinking we can get us some stripper stuff and a few extra screws and make them pieces shine like they were meant to do."

"You mean repair antiques? I have no idea how to do that. I mean, I can fix a few things around the house if I have to, but I don't know the first thing about repairing old furniture." Grandda nodded but was smiling. "I'm willing to help, but I don't know what I'd be doing."

"You can learn, can't you? I mean, you learned how to tell people to have safe words and how to love a woman while lashing her to a big piece of wood, didn't you? You even know all about them fancy knots that they tie them up in. You learned that fairly easy. I'm just asking you to learn a few things with me." Scott nearly drove them off the road when his grandda laughed. "Yes, I know what you did. And how you had to do most of it too. You don't think I'd just blindly let my grandsons do a job without knowing a little about it, do you?"

"I didn't know. I mean, I knew you had an idea, but that's all." Scott drove more carefully as he thought of his grandda's request for help. When he told him to park in front of a large building, something else occurred to him. "You already started, didn't you?"

"Yeah. If I had to wait on you to make a decision, I might be cold in my grave by then." Scott started to tell him that wasn't going to happen when he remembered that Trent said to wait a few days or a few thousand years to tell them they were immortal too. "Come on in, we'll have a looksee around."

He had to admit after seeing the ideas that Grandda was telling him about, Scott was excited. They would have two floors, the upper levels for a show room kind of deal and the lower floor to work in. He said that having the customers see what they were doing would impress them more when they saw the goods. There was even an office on the second floor complete with a desk that looked like the one his dad had found and given to Noelle for her business. As they made their way around, looking at the large windows that weren't broken and the furnace that would need to be replaced soon, he thought of what it would be like to work with his hands again. He'd done a little glass trimming when he'd been a teenager. Some of the nicer homes in town still had some of the stained glass lamps and windows that he had helped build.

"I'll do it." His grandda whooped and yelled when Scott told him he would be his partner. And to celebrate, they decided to have dinner in town, just the two of them. Scott thought that perhaps he might even start glass working again, just to fill in the time between the pieces of furniture. And he was sure there would be plenty of time too. Who had furniture stripped anymore?

Now Available in the Calhoun Men Series

Trent
Calhoun Men Book 1

Elijah
Calhoun Men Book 2

Before You Go...

HELP AN AUTHOR

write a review

THANK YOU!

Share your voice and help guide other readers to these wonderful books. Even if it's only a line or two your reviews help readers discover the author's books so they can continue creating stories that you'll love. Login to your favorite retailer and leave a review. Thank you.

AWARD WINNING, BESTSELLING AUTHOR

Kathi Barton, winner of the Pinnacle Book Achievement award as well as a best-selling author on Amazon and All Romance books, lives in Nashport, Ohio with her husband Paul. When not creating new worlds and romance, Kathi and her husband enjoy camping and going to auctions. She can also be seen at county fairs with her husband who is an artist and potter.

Her muse, a cross between Jimmy Stewart and Hugh Jackman, brings her stories to life for her readers in a way that has them coming back time and again for more. Her favorite genre is paranormal romance with a great deal of spice. You can visit Kathi on line and drop her an email if you'd like. She loves hearing from her fans. aaronskiss@gmail.com.

Follow Kathi on her blog:
http://kathisbartonauthor.blogspot.com/

www.ingramcontent.com/pod-product-compliance
Lightning Source LLC
Chambersburg PA
CBHW032130170626
46808CB00006B/2170